Peter Buckman was o
publishing and is now c
still practising. In betw
producing books, play
and radio, articles ar

Mysteries are his first crime series, and feature a quartet of characters in their seventies (including the dog) who are still working, still learning, and still enjoying life with all its problems. Peter and his wife Rosie have lived in the same Oxfordshire village for over fifty years; they have two daughters, two grandchildren, and a black cockerpoo called, amazingly, Pumpernickel.

The Pumpernickel Mysteries

Dead Early

Dead Honest

Dead Rich

Dead Famous

Dead Religious

Dead Unpopular

Dead Festive (novella)

DEAD FESTIVE

Peter Buckman

WORD OF MOUTH BOOKS

ISBN 978-1-0683333-6-1

Cover design by Peter O'Connor.

Logo design by Alan Mauro.

Published by Word of Mouth Books.

Dead Festive

Julian held up three callused fingers. He was a builder, and the paper crown from his Christmas cracker sat askew on his shaven head.

'Three words,' Leo said. He was well pleased with the way his vegetarian Wellington had turned out: everyone said it was far better than a turkey, even his old friend Dennis, who was more interested in wine than food, and surreptitiously filled his glass when his wife Susan wasn't looking. Leo smiled. The Stilton was on the table, they were having a pause before the Christmas pudding and mince pies, which Leo hadn't made himself: Marion had insisted on buying them from Fortnum's. She said Leo had more than enough to do, catering for her brother Harold and his partner Julian. Who now held up two fingers.

'Second word,' Marion said. She was not someone who cared about appearances, but she'd made a special effort and was wearing a white linen shirt over a pair of powder-blue corduroys. Leo thought she looked terrific, her ruddy complexion with her dyed purple hair and lilac paper hat having the colours of a winter sunset. He smiled lovingly at her. She beamed back.

Julian pointed a finger at himself.

'Chest?' Susan suggested. She was quite merry on the port, and her pleasure in playing charades more than compensated for her husband's disapproval.

'Poof!' Harold said. He was a couple of years younger than his sister, so the same age as Leo, who was meeting him for the first time since he and Marion got together. Harold was a jovial bearded man who could have played Father Christmas, except he was wearing a flowery dress, a very blingy bracelet and white court shoes.

Julian wagged his finger at Harold, shook his head, adjusted his paper hat, then pointed at Dennis and Leo in turn.

'Man!' Leo's granddaughter Jazz said. She was supposed to have gone skiing over Christmas but had fractured a toe playing football. Her parents were on a yoga retreat in Wales so Jazz, whose real name was Jasmine, had accepted Leo's invitation to join them, which had lowered the average age of the party considerably.

Julian nodded enthusiastically. Then he held up three fingers.

'Third word,' Leo said. He sneaked a look at his watch. His younger sister Becky and her husband Graham were going to drop by with their moody son Jonathan, and Leo was worried there wouldn't be enough mince pies. But nothing could be done about that now: it was Christmas Day, after all.

Julian took three paces to his left, turned, and took three to his right.

'Exercise!' Susan said.

'Don't be silly, Susan,' Dennis said. He was a large man who overflowed his chair; he had refused to wear a crown, and only the presence of Marion, and her excellent wine, prevented him from being thoroughly disagreeable. Despite being Leo's oldest friend, there were times when he behaved like a grumpy in-law who was there because he couldn't be left on his own.

'Why would a man need exercise?' he continued. 'Unless he is confined in some way. Such as in prison.'

Julian made beckoning gestures of encouragement.

'What does that mean?' Dennis asked. 'Does he want me to join him? Is he inviting me to dance?'

Harold laughed so much he almost choked. Marion had to bang him on the back. 'Julian, dance?' he said, when he'd recovered. 'We went to a birthday ball in the Brighton Pavilion, and he trod on the hem of my organza, which tore right up to my knickers. Luckily I'd shaved my legs!'

Julian shook his head and repeated his pacing.

'Steps?' Leo asked. 'Paces? Manspace?'

Pumpernickel, Leo's black poodle, who had been sitting watching Julian's performance with a bemused expression, gave a short bark of encouragement. Or it may have been criticism. Or boredom. So far nobody had dropped any Stilton, which was disappointing. He'd had a bit of the crust of Leo's pastry, which the dog thought tasted better than the beetroot and mushroom filling, and had been looking forward to the cheese course. But they were all too busy playing their silly game. He got up and ambled over to Jazz. She was his friend and ally. He pushed his nose against her shin.

'Careful, Pumpy!' she said. 'That's my bad leg. I wanted them to wrap it in plaster, so that everyone could see how much I was suffering, but they don't do that anymore. You want some cheese, don't you?' She broke off a crumb from the slice on her plate, and put it on the floor. Pumpernickel growled appreciatively, then lay down to examine the cheese carefully. He wasn't one of those dogs who scoff anything that comes their way. He was discriminating and quite fussy about his food, like Leo. Unlike Leo, though, he always knew when he'd had enough.

Julian stamped his foot and did three more paces, to the left and the right.

'Stomp?' Harold said. 'Or are you getting in a fret? It serves you right for locking yourself in the lavatory before. You thought you'd escaped playing charades, but you didn't get away with it, did you?' Julian pouted at him, then ambled around his chair.

'Walking!' Jazz said. Julian raised both his thumbs. Leo clapped his clever granddaughter. She'd won a scholarship to Balliol College, Oxford, to read History, and she deserved encouragement. And needed it, too: her mother Tina seemed to disapprove of her going to such an elitist institution, never mind her spending time on things like rowing and beagling, not that that stopped Jazz from seriously enjoying herself. Leo was convinced Tina was secretly proud of her daughter but refused to let it show. For which he blamed himself: when he and his ex-wife Deirdre had gone their separate ways after ten years of marriage, Tina had stayed with her mother. She had accepted her father's weekend visits and accompanied him dutifully, but without enthusiasm, when he took her out, mostly to his sister's, as he thought she'd enjoy mingling with her boisterous cousins. Leo still wanted Tina's approval – at least she got on well with Marion, though who didn't? – but he was free to adore Jazz, who treated him with the loving disrespect he deserved.

Julian raised one finger – 'First word,' Susan pointed out helpfully – then he lay down on the ancient but valuable Persian carpet that Marion's father had bought to impress his mistress when he had installed her in the mansion flat his daughter had inherited after he'd died. Julian's paper crown fell off, but he ignored it. He crossed his arms across his chest and closed his eyes.

'Sleeping beauty!' Harold said.

'Let sleeping dogs lie?' Dennis suggested, drinking more wine.

'No, dear,' Susan said patiently. 'The other words were...'

'Dead man walking!' Jazz said triumphantly.

'Brilliant!' Leo said. 'Your turn next!'

'Well done, Jazz!' Marion said. 'But you don't have to do one if you don't want to.'

'Don't say that!' Harold said. 'Julian didn't want to play, but he did, in the end, didn't he?'

'You know how I hated being made to act in the school play, Harold,' Marion said. 'Though that may be to do with the fact that I was always cast as a great galumphing villain, bloody Tybalt, for example, when I rather fancied myself as Juliet.'

'You would have made a perfectly splendid Juliet, dear lady,' Dennis said unctuously. 'And the fact that you do not force your guests to disport themselves in roles they might find unpalatable is a sign of your discrimination and excellent sense. Which has only failed you when you unaccountably picked my friend Leo as your partner. You

11

could have done so much better, dear lady, and I'm confident that you will!'

'I love Leo,' Susan said. 'I would happily have married him when he was your best man, but he didn't ask me.'

'Dennis got in first,' Leo said gallantly. 'All this,' he turned to explain to Harold, 'was many years before I met your sister. Who is the best thing that ever happened to me.' He reached out a hand to squeeze Marion's.

'Certainly a lot better than you deserve,' Dennis said.

'She scrubs up quite nicely, doesn't she?' Harold said. 'You should have seen her when we were kids. She had the dress sense of a camel!'

'I didn't have much choice, did I?' Marion retorted. 'You wore all my clothes!'

'Yes,' Harold agreed, 'but I looked so much better in them. Julian, dear, you can get up now. We got it, dear. Well, Jazz did: isn't she a clever little thing?'

Julian didn't move.

Harold said, 'Julian?'

Everyone turned to look at Julian. Who still didn't move.

Pumpernickel went over and sniffed him. Then he barked. A warning bark.

Marion got up from her seat at the big round table and approached the inert Julian. She bent down and picked up one of his hands. The other arm flopped to his side. Marion put two fingers on his neck to feel for a pulse. She straightened up, her broad round face looking serious.

'I rather think,' she said, 'that he's dead. We'd better call emergency services.'

Harold shuddered all over. 'Are you sure?' he said.

'She is a doctor,' Leo said reassuringly. Not quite knowing what else to do, he filled everyone's glass.

'Not of the medical kind,' Harold said, automatically gulping wine while keeping his eyes on his supine partner. 'He could be shamming. I'm sure I saw his chest move.'

'I don't think so, sweetie,' Marion said gently. 'I'll call 999. Though it will be a while before they come, I

13

imagine. I'll get a sheet to cover him. We'd better not move him, had we?'

'He looks so peaceful, doesn't he?' Susan said. 'Did he have a dicky heart?'

'Strong as an ox,' Harold said, still gazing at the body.

'I've never seen a corpse before,' Jazz announced. 'Well, not a human one, anyway. What happens to a body when it dies? I skipped biology.'

'I really don't think this is a suitable time to discuss the loosening of the bladder and bowel,' Dennis said. This was familiar territory to him – he had awarded himself the byline 'the world's most fearless crime reporter' – and he relished the opportunity to take charge. 'We should be grateful our friend Julian spent so much time in the loo before his last appearance. The first thing my friends in the police service will want to establish is what he died of. The second is why.'

'It could be an embolism, dear,' Susan said. 'Or an aneurysm. Or a brain haemorrhage: my aunt Lucy died of one of those. Came back from bingo, sat in her chair, and pouf! And she'd won a bottle of brandy in the raffle!'

'Talking of which,' Leo said, 'would anyone like a brandy while we're waiting? It's supposed to help with the shock, isn't it? Though with the amount of booze we've got through, it's no wonder we're all a bit numbed.'

'I suppose it could be food poisoning,' Dennis remarked. 'Leo's culinary expertise is something he has only acquired late in life. Though he was renowned for many things in his younger days, the provision of palatable food was not among them.'

'You mean, like poisonous mushrooms?' Jazz said. 'Gramps wouldn't do that! He and Pumpy don't go foraging in fields, do they, though I'm sure Pumps would make a good truffle hound.' She rubbed the dog's head affectionately. He yawned and shook himself. The atmosphere in the room was veering from conviviality to uncertainty, and he wasn't sure how to deal with it. At least Jazz was acting normally.

'He's never been the sort of grandfather who'd take me birdwatching or tree-hugging,' she continued. 'A football match, yes. A walk round Kew Gardens, no. When he goes hunting, it's for bargains in Sainsbury's.'

'Waitrose, actually,' Leo said. 'And Berwick Street market.'

'If there was anything wrong with the food,' Marion said, 'we'd all be feeling it, wouldn't we? I'll make the call and fetch the brandy. Or would you rather have something else, Harold? Do you still like Kummel? There's probably an old bottle of Dad's somewhere!' She went out of the room.

Harold shook his head, dislodging his paper hat. He couldn't take his eyes off Julian, though he smoothed and folded the hat mechanically. 'I can't believe it,' he said. 'I don't believe it. I don't want to believe it.'

He suddenly lurched to his feet and tottered over to the body. He put the back of his hand on Julian's cheek, then whipped it away as if stung. 'Still warm!' he said. Pumpernickel came up to him and whined sympathetically. Harold bent his head and sobbed. Everyone shifted uncomfortably in their chair. Pumpernickel stayed close to Harold and licked his hand.

'Thank you,' Harold said, patting his head. 'That's just what I needed.' He straightened up, smoothed his skirt, returned to his place at the table, jiggled his bracelet back down his wrist and picked up his glass.

'Well!' he said. 'Christmas with your family: you always expect the worst, don't you? What do we do now?'

'We wait,' Dennis said, 'and we drink.' He took a big swallow, and reached towards the bottle. Susan moved it out of his reach.

'What are you doing?' he demanded.

'I think you should take it easy, dear,' Susan said. 'If only out of respect.'

'Julian no longer cares if I drink or I don't,' Dennis retorted. 'I shall respect him just as much with more of this excellent wine as I did before. More, in fact, as I am no fan of amateur dramatics. The amount I drink has no effect on my mental acuity: my capacity is legendary. I could drink anyone here present under the table, with the possible exception of our fair hostess, whose reputation for hard-headedness I have yet to put to the test. Perhaps,' he continued as Marion returned with a folded sheet, 'now is the very time to do so.'

He took advantage of Susan being distracted by grabbing the bottle and filling his glass.

'Somebody will come,' Marion announced, 'but they don't know when.' She started to unfold the sheet, but Harold put out his braceleted arm.

'Don't,' he said. 'I want to see his face for a bit longer. No one minds, do they?' He looked around the table. 'I mean, as Susan said, he looks so peaceful. You'd think he was just having a nap, wouldn't you? It would be just like him to stretch out in front of a fire – very keen on open fireplaces, was Julian – and close his little eyes.'

Everyone mumbled their acceptance. Marion dropped the sheet on the floor and resumed her seat. Jazz leant forward.

'What was he like?' she asked. 'How did you meet?'

'Well,' Harold said, swirling wine around his glass, 'he came to give a quote for putting in a new bathroom and doing a bit of a refurb. I run this lovely guest house in Hove – long-term residents, none of that Airbnb nonsense: they've ruined it for everyone – and one of my ladies died, in her bed, as it happens, so you might

18

say I'm accustomed to sudden departures.' He waved a hand in Julian's direction, then picked up a plate and thrust it in Jazz's direction.

'Can you give me some of that cheese, dear?' he asked. 'I think the shock has made me hungry.'

'There's plenty more,' Leo said, 'and we haven't even started on the mince pies and pudding.'

'I thought we were waiting for your sister, sweetie,' Marion said.

'We don't have to,' Leo said. 'Who was to know one of us was going to drop dead during the course of the afternoon? I'm not sure what the done thing is in these circumstances – I dare say Dennis will tell us – but we should try and stay calm, and to me that means being fed and watered. If Harold's hungry...'

'The Stilton will do me, for now,' Harold said, accepting a generous portion from Jazz, who took another slice herself, and dropped some for Pumpernickel, who showed his gratitude by wagging his feathery tail.

'Go on about Julian,' Jazz said. Marion gave her an approving look. As a practising therapist, she encouraged people to talk about whatever or whoever was bothering them. It was a lot better than bottling up your feelings and avoiding the subject. Though Julian was hard to avoid when he was lying there in the middle of the room, dead.

'Well,' Harold said, 'I didn't take to him at all, at first. Rufty tufty types have never appealed to me, especially if they have dirty fingernails. And he had the most appalling combover you have ever seen!'

'Forgive me,' Dennis said, 'but what exactly is a combover?'

'How can you not know what a combover is?' Leo said. 'It's when you try and disguise your bald patch by letting what's left of your hair grow long enough to cover it. It never works, especially if there's a wind. And it's not like you to sound like a doddery old judge.'

'Though my areas of ignorance are nowhere near as extensive as yours,' Dennis retorted, 'I am never afraid to enquire. It's better than pretending, as you do, to knowledge you do not possess.'

Pumpernickel sighed. Susan echoed him. 'Now, boys,' she said, 'no bickering. You can save all that for your regular lunchtime sessions in the pub. Let Harold carry on.'

Harold glanced over at Julian, then popped some cheese into his mouth. 'But,' he said, 'he didn't do what most builders do, you know, suck his teeth and say, "What cowboy did you get to do this, then?" He was actually quite complimentary about the way I'd kept the old features, and he liked what I wanted to do with the bathroom. Plus his quote was the middle one, and you should always take that, shouldn't you? Not the cheapest, because you get what you pay for, nor the most expensive, even if it does come from a firm with a posh reputation. Though he had a good reputation too: several of the ladies I play bridge with raved about him, to such an extent I thought he must be doing more than sorting out their plumbing. But it turned out he wasn't that way inclined. Which I only discovered when I bumped into him at an exhibition devoted to the work of Derek Jarman. You know who I mean?'

Dennis opened his mouth, but Susan forestalled him. 'I loved *Caravaggio*,' she said, 'and he was a good painter too.'

'I didn't know you enjoyed such things, Susan,' Dennis said disparagingly.

'You don't know what I get up to while you're writing about criminals and degenerates,' Susan said lightly. 'My life isn't all shopping and book clubs, you know!'

'I would never assume...' Dennis began, only to be interrupted by Jazz.

'How long have you and Julian been together?' she asked Harold. Who drank a little more while considering the question.

'Do you know, I'm not sure?' he said. 'Two years? Three? Time thunders by when you're older, doesn't it? He wasn't around when you last paid me the honour of a visit, was he, Marion? So busy I hardly see you! I only found out you'd met the love of your life when you scrawled it on a birthday card! Which arrived late, by the way.'

'I know, Harold,' Marion said, patting his hand. 'I'm a terrible sister. I take the blame for everything, just like I always did.'

'I never said that,' Harold objected. 'You were very good with Mother. She never spoke, you know,' he explained to the rest of the company. 'She left little notes.'

'Some people,' Dennis observed, 'might regard a silent parent as a blessing. It would allow for considerable latitude in behaviour. A written note can be interpreted in any number of ways.'

'When my mum goes silent,' Jazz said, 'Dad and I tremble.'

'Your mother is a law unto herself,' Leo said, 'and that's probably my fault. When your grandmother and I finally parted...'

'Deirdre was as much to blame as you were, Leo,' Susan said. 'She gave you a hard time even before she went demented. The way she carried on at those wild parties! I was quite intimidated by her.'

'You exaggerate, Susan,' Dennis said. 'You had, of course, led rather a sheltered life prior to our meeting – she was a member of the typing pool on the paper where I was a reporter with several scoops to my name,' he explained to the rest of the table. 'This was when our host Leo was still an inky-fingered student of the law clad in flowery shirts and flares that were too tight for him, who couldn't hold his drink and dissolved into giggles whenever a joint came his way.'

'Hold on a minute!' Jazz said. 'You, Dennis, went in for drink and drugs and rock and roll?'

'In my youth,' Dennis said, 'I sampled everything that was on offer. Except hard drugs: I was never one for those. Nor, I may say, was your grandfather. He used to insist we were part of a revolution that would change the world, but for me, it was a time for hedonism, and I was a hedonist. I still enjoy my drink; your grandfather still clings to the notion that goodness will prevail over villainy. I chronicle villainy all the time, and I leave it to you to decide whose vision of life is more accurate.'

Pumpernickel, who had heard this many times, sighed heavily. The rest digested Dennis's sentiments in silence. Which was broken by a sudden burst of the Beatles' song 'Let It Be'. It came from a mobile phone.

Everyone patted their pockets, then looked around to locate the sound. There was no doubt of its source. Julian. The phone was visible, tucked into his trousers. And the music still played.

24

Harold said, 'Don't answer it!'

Marion said, 'We can't just let it ring, Harold!'

'I beg to disagree with you, dear lady,' Dennis said, 'but police procedure...'

'Dennis!' Susan said sharply. 'It might explain why he died!'

'I suppose,' Leo said, 'it wouldn't do any harm to pick it up. Any prints would be Julian's, and the cops will only be interested in what's on it. Isn't that right, Dennis?'

'We can at least vouchsafe that Julian did not use it in our presence,' Dennis said. 'Though perhaps he made a call when he was – otherwise occupied. He was gone for quite a while.'

With an encouraging look from Marion, Leo got up and went over to the body. He gingerly extracted the still ringing phone from Julian's trouser pocket. He attempted to silence it by stabbing at the screen. Being a klutz where technology was concerned, he handed it to Jazz. The moment she took it, it stopped ringing.

'It's gone to voicemail,' she said. She fiddled with it, then found the right icons and pressed the speaker button so they could all listen.

Instead of a message, there was a lot of shouting, and a woman with a strong accent said, 'Bracelet? You have it?' A man said, 'Dead, I told you,' and then there was more shouting and a crashing sound. After which the phone went silent.

'Fuck!' Harold said. He reached for his drink. His hand trembled.

'Isn't that what they refer to as a pocket call?' Leo asked, returning to his seat. 'You know, when you accidentally hit a key and it connects with someone you never meant to speak to?'

'Must be,' Harold said quickly.

'Were the voices familiar to you, Harold?' Dennis asked.

Marion said, 'It's alright, sweetie. You're among friends. Do you know who that was?'

Harold drank, put down his glass, adjusted his dress, smoothed his hair, and said, 'How could I tell? How could anyone tell? Whoever they were, they were having a fight, weren't they? It must be a mistake!'

'The word "bracelet" was mentioned,' Dennis said. 'By a woman with a pronounced accent.'

'East European,' Leo said. 'I could hear that, even with these blasted things in.' He fiddled with his hearing aids.

'That's what I thought,' Susan said. 'Hungarian, possibly? Or Russian? Maybe Ukrainian – one of our book club members...'

'Putting aside, for the moment, the origin of the caller,' Dennis interrupted impatiently, 'and assuming that the call was indeed intended for Julian, why would she enquire about a bracelet?'

They all looked at Harold, who combed his white beard with his fingers and eventually said, 'I don't know! Julian never talked much about his work. He said he liked to forget it when he came home, and lose himself in my little world of bridge and Febreze and sandwiches with the crusts cut off.'

'What has Febreze to do with this case?' Dennis demanded. 'What is it?'

'An air freshener, dear,' Susan said. 'You can also use it to tiddle up sheets that have only been slept in once. It saves on washing and ironing, dear, but you wouldn't know about that.'

'Thank you, Susan,' Harold said. 'I'm glad someone here understands the demands of domesticity.'

'I understand all that,' Jazz said, 'though I thought you only had sandwiches with the crusts cut off at society weddings. Which I've only been to one of. But surely, Harold, you must have some idea of who Julian was working for? It's pretty hard to keep secrets from someone you love and live with, isn't it? I know I couldn't, but I tend to blab about everything anyway. Just like Gramps.'

'I do not blab!' Leo protested. 'I admit I am not good with secrets...'

'If one wants something broadcast, one only has to tell it to you in confidence,' Dennis said.

'But he's very good at client confidentiality,' Marion said. 'And you were rubbish at keeping secrets as a boy, dear Harold. Remember when Micky Pond told you about his parents' porn collection? You chatted merrily about it at one of Dad's cocktail parties, and they never got asked again.'

'Julian didn't share secrets with me!' Harold wailed. 'I wasn't aware he had any. There are some relationships, aren't there, where you don't want to know too much, you just accept things as they are, because...I don't know, you can't believe your luck. The more you know, the more you worry, don't you? I didn't want it to end because of some grubby little revelation!'

'Maybe it's not a revelation, Harold,' Leo said soothingly, filling his guest's glass. 'Maybe it's a clue that'll help us understand what, if anything, is going on. Of course this is difficult for you – it's difficult for all of us, believe me! But we're all on your side, so anything you can remember, anything you can tell us...'

'He had a fondness for chocolate champagne truffles,' Harold said. 'Will that do? He tried to hide them from me, because I quite like them myself.'

'Was he good at concealing them?' Dennis demanded.

'Why does that matter?' Susan asked.

'Because,' Dennis said, 'if you hide something from someone you live with, it's a sign you don't trust them.'

'I hide things all the time,' Susan said. 'But not from you – if there was something you couldn't find, you'd just shout for me, wouldn't you? I hide things I don't want to bother with, like clothes that need mending, or little surprises for the children, whom I trust absolutely.'

'Perhaps,' Marion said mildly, 'Julian didn't want to burden you, dear Harold, with anything that might put you in danger. Because he cared about you and wanted to protect you.'

'Champagne truffles?' Harold said. 'What harm could they do, apart from to the hips? I always thought I was the protective one. He shaved his head when I persuaded him to get rid of the combover, and he had a little tattoo done on his buttock – a secret sunflower, because I love sunflowers – but a trumpery bit of costume jewellery? Why would anyone be interested in that?'

He tried to push his bracelet under the sleeve of his dress, which naturally drew everyone's attention to it.

Leo said, gently, 'They did mention it on the phone, didn't they?'

Harold sighed.

'Alright,' he said. 'We did have a tiny row about it. I can't imagine what it has to do with that phone call, but still.' He picked up his glass. 'It was last week,' he said. 'I was tidying up our bedroom when I noticed something sticking out of Julian's drawer, the one in his bedside table. I pulled it open to shut it properly, if you know what I mean, and I saw this.' He shook his free hand so the bracelet slid into view. He held it up so they could all see it.

'It's very – you should excuse me, but – kitsch, isn't it?' Leo said.

'I think it's amazing,' Jazz said.

'A little, ah, flashy for my taste,' Dennis said, 'but each to their own.'

'It's so vulgar, it's gorgeous!' Harold said. 'And the first thing I asked myself was, what's Julian doing with it? My second thought was, it's just the thing to wear to Marion's Christmas lunch. It'll knock her socks off!'

'Just having you here is enough for me,' Marion said. 'You know you don't have to dress to impress.'

Harold swallowed some wine. 'To be honest,' he said, 'I was a little nervous. Mainly about bringing Julian. Not that I'm ashamed of him, or anything – far from it: he's the best thing that's happened to me in years!'

'Like your sister is to me,' Leo said quietly. Marion flashed him a smile, Pumpernickel made a throaty noise of approval and support.

'I knew Marion would be fine,' Harold went on, 'but this is the first time I've met Leo, never mind his friends...'

'Dennis is much more tolerant than he pretends,' Susan said. 'I wouldn't have stayed with him otherwise.'

'Yes, well,' Harold said, 'I suppose I wanted to be the centre of attention, in case Julian felt intimidated. Even though it's only a bit of costume jewellery, it goes rather well with my dress, don't you think?'

There were polite murmurs of agreement. Then Jazz asked, 'What was it doing in Julian's drawer?'

'That's exactly what I wanted to know,' Harold said. 'All sorts of suspicions crossed my mind – who would give him such a thing? had he stolen it? – and you know how once you start worrying, you get more and more twisted up. I'm not normally one for confrontation. Ask my sister how much I hate rows!'

He turned to Marion for confirmation. She nodded sympathetically.

'And especially,' Harold continued, 'with people I care about. I didn't want a row with Julian. We loved each other: why would I risk all that?' He looked over to the body and drank some more. Nobody moved, not even Pumpernickel.

'So I asked him,' Harold went on. 'I put it on the table in our living room, by the fruit bowl, not where it would be too obvious, but you couldn't miss a thing like this, could you?' He jangled the bracelet so that its stones caught the light. 'I practised being casual.' He put on an artificially soft voice. '"I was just tidying up and look what I found!" But what came out, the moment he saw it, was, "Where did you get that, then?"'

He stopped and blew his nose elaborately. Leo leant forward. 'So what did he say?' he asked.

'He looked from it to me,' Harold said, 'and told me it was a present. "Who from?" I asked him. He dropped his eyes, and I thought, Uh-oh, this is it. It's all over. Why did I have to find the damn thing? Why couldn't I just pretend I hadn't seen it?'

'You were always good at pretending, Harold,' Marion said softly.

'But this was real!' Harold said. He glanced at Julian and shook his head to clear it. 'Anyway,' he said, 'he looked me full in the face, and said, "From me to you. Happy Christmas!" How do you answer that?' He emptied his glass and held it out to Leo for a refill.

'Did you enquire where he obtained it?' Dennis asked, also holding out his glass. Leo filled them both up.

'You don't ask things like that, Dennis!' Susan said. 'If someone you love gives you a present you love, you accept it gratefully!'

'Exactly, Susan!' Harold said. 'I was so relieved, I threw my arms around him. He was a little embarrassed, to be honest. He mumbled something about getting it from this Russian he was working for, some billionaire with a grand house near Rottingdean, and it was so over the top, he thought of me. The cheek of it!' He turned his wrist this way and that, admiring the jewels. 'Of course it's fake,' he concluded. 'He might have got it in the Lanes, for all I know. But I was happy with his story. It is rather me, I'm sorry to say!'

'There nothing fake about you, Harold,' Leo said heartily. 'I like your story!'

'It does not, however, explain either the telephone call or Julian's sudden demise,' Dennis said.

'They could both be accidental,' Susan said.

'They will nevertheless have to be investigated,' Dennis said. 'The police will treat this as a suspicious death.'

'Poor Julian,' Susan said. 'Everyone's suspicious about builders, I suppose. They're like plumbers, or electricians: they promise you the world, they take your deposit, they swear they'll show up next Monday at eight o'clock sharp, and you don't see them for weeks! Months, even. The nagging drives you mad!'

'Did he say anything more about the Russian he was working for, Harold?' Leo asked. 'Did he mention any problems between them? I try not to burden your sister with the problems my clients land me with – Pumpy gets more of an earful than she does – but sometimes you just have to share with the person you care about more than anyone else in the world!'

The dog sat up on hearing his name, but there seemed to be no immediate demand for his services. Jazz tossed him another bit of Stilton, which he swallowed before stretching out at her feet with his head between his paws.

'You never did have much in the way of self-control,' Dennis remarked to Leo. 'It's a miracle you and Deirdre stayed together for as long as you did.'

'You've had your lapses too, dear. Remember?' Susan said, helping herself to more port. 'That time when you were involved with the Russian ballerina? I did consider leaving, only Felicity was still at primary school.'

'I was ensnared in what in police circles is known as a honey trap, Susan, because my writing about the involvement of Russian criminal elements with certain leading politicians was getting too close to the mark. At no point did I act with impropriety.'

'I suppose being seen entering strip clubs on the arm of a Russian dancer doesn't count as improper,' Susan said, without malice.

Leo was about to comment on this insight into the life of his oldest friend when Harold said, 'Now you mention Russians, I'd been on at Julian to change the taps in the second-floor en suite, and he came back with these gilded things that were far too flashy for a three-quarter length avocado bath with attached shower. I asked if they had fallen off a lorry, and he got quite stroppy, Julian, which wasn't like him at all. Such a silly little thing to quarrel about. If only I'd known!'

Jazz said, 'What's that got to do with a Russian?'

'Good question,' Leo said. 'Should I open another bottle?'

'That,' Dennis said, drinking, 'is the most sensible suggestion I've heard you make in a while.'

Marion said, 'Go on, Harold. Did the gold taps come from the Russian oligarch?'

'I didn't know that then,' Harold said.

'Those of us not stricken by grief,' Dennis commented, 'though of course we are all concerned at the demise of someone who so recently attempted to keep us entertained, would have made the same assumption as our hostess.'

'What?' Harold said, looking confused.

'He means we think Julian nicked the taps from his Russian client,' Leo said. 'So did he?'

'He did not nick things!' Harold said defensively. 'Julian was as honest as...well, as honest as anyone can be in our dishonest world. The Russian gave him the taps because they weren't blingy enough. He wanted solid gold, apparently, not gold-plated. Julian installed them – it was the last little job he did in the house, now I come to think of it.'

He started to look tearful again. Marion said, 'What we heard on his phone: could that have been the same Russian?'

'How would I know?' Harold said dolefully. 'I never spoke to the man, I never met him, as far as I'm

38

aware. The only Russian I know is a former grandmaster at chess who somebody said was thrown out by the International Federation or whatever it is for cheating. She may have been very good at playing with pawns, but her bidding at bridge is impossible!'

'If it wasn't the taps,' Jazz said, helping herself to some of the port Susan was drinking, 'why else would whoever made that phone call mention that someone was dead?'

They all looked at Julian's phone, which Jazz had put down on the table, as if it was a grenade that might go off at any moment.

'Maybe it's a crime of passion,' Leo said, 'over some affair Julian, bless him, was having, or may have had in the past, before he found Harold.'

'I fear the toil of catering for these festivities has softened what is left of your mind,' Dennis remarked. 'Not, of course, that it was ever particularly acute. It would take the rose-coloured view of an incurable romantic to believe that an unrequited passion lies behind a premature and untimely death – which, as my wife has pointed out, might not be in the least suspicious: we will not be able to ascertain the true cause until a pathologist has examined the corpse.'

Harold started to sob. Susan said, 'You might try and be a little more tactful, dear. Harold has lost his partner: he doesn't need you pontificating!'

'I was merely...'

'What if it was someone who was jealous of Harold?' Leo suggested. 'A past lover of Julian's, a bad loser at bridge, some old fart who resents the way Harold swans around with his beard and his dresses, which his friends and family accept because it makes him happy and he looks so good in them?'

Harold sniffed, then preened himself a little. 'Do you really think so?' he asked.

'Of course you do,' Marion said briskly. 'There's no need to fish for compliments. But Leo has a point. Do you know anyone in Julian's past who might still be in love with him?'

'He and I have been an item for so long...'

'How long is "so long"?' Leo asked. 'Your sister and I have been together for five years, but it seems only yesterday I answered her ad in *Private Eye*. Love makes you lose all count of time.'

'Yuk, Gramps!' Jazz said. 'Can we concentrate on Harold and Julian?'

'I second your granddaughter's stricture,' Dennis said. 'If we are to succumb to saccharine sentimentality...'

'When you get all alliterative,' Leo said, nettled, 'it's a sure sign you have nothing useful to say.'

Pumpernickel barked. 'Quite right, Pumps,' Jazz said. 'Someone has to keep order here. What do you reckon, Harold? Can you think of anybody?'

'There is someone, as a matter of fact,' Harold said. 'They made it quite clear they would be happy to have Julian patching up their plaster on a permanent basis. Very disappointed, they were, when his van became a permanent feature outside my house. They were so put out they stopped coming to play bridge for three whole weeks, but in the end they couldn't resist my coffee and walnut.'

'Are you saying that a concupiscent bridge player...' Dennis began.

'A what?'

'That one of your acquaintances,' Dennis continued, 'was driven by lust and jealousy so strong that he arranged the assassination of your partner, in your sister's apartments, on Christmas Day?' He shook his head disbelievingly. 'I have been covering criminal matters for a considerable time – over half a century, in fact – and I have to tell you, with the greatest respect, that such an idea would stretch the most generous credulity!' He emptied his glass, put it down, and folded his arms across his broad chest as if awaiting further explanation. There was a short silence, but Harold was not cowed.

'It isn't a "he",' he said disarmingly. 'Her name is Selma Day, she was an actress in her time, though they call themselves actors now, don't they? Anyway, she was quite successful, or pretty or beddable enough to attract a number of wealthy gentlemen, at least two of whom married her one after the other, leaving her nicely off, thank you very much, with a big house in the same street where Larry Olivier ended up with that nice little Joan Plowright.'

Dennis nodded, refilled his glass, then said, in a milder tone, 'But what, forgive me asking, would this Selma Day want with Julian? I assure you I am not blinkered or prejudiced when it comes to sexual predilections, but you surely would not expect me, or the investigating officers when they arrive, to take seriously the notion that a wealthy widow would harbour a passion for a person of the homosexual persuasion so deep it would lead her to murder!'

Susan said, to the table in general, 'You have to make allowances for him, you know. He wasn't like this when I married him. He was lean and hungry and unsure of himself, but all that's been swallowed up in blubber. You don't notice it happening when you live with someone day in, day out, do you? It's only on occasions like this, when a shock makes you realize what they've become. But he's still a good man, and not a bad writer, and I'm still quite fond of him, though you mustn't take him too seriously.'

'Susan!' Dennis protested. 'Is this the port talking? I cannot believe...'

'Many women are attracted to gay men, as a matter of fact,' Marion said. 'I've been something of a fag hag myself, before Leo, of course. This Selma Day might well have found Julian irresistible after two husbands who presumably married her for her physical charms. I can understand her resenting Harold's presence – an actor is accustomed to praise and attention, and to see Julian's affection concentrated on my brother might have been galling – but whether brooding on that would have led her to murder the man she fancied: that's something a detective will have to unravel.'

Leo filled her glass. 'I agree,' he said. 'Though until the cops arrive, we can speculate, can't we? Tell us more about Selma, Harold. Is she really insanely jealous?'

'Even if she is,' Dennis said, holding out his glass for more, 'and even if we grant that she harboured strong feelings for Julian – which, despite my wife's extraordinary outburst, I concede is entirely possible, especially after Marion's illuminating history – how would an actress who is presumably ensconced in her Regency house in Brighton engineer the death of a rival enjoying a festive repast, even a vegetarian one, in a secure mansion flat overlooking Hyde Park?'

'Could she have sent Julian a message via his phone that could trigger a fatal heart attack?' Leo wondered.

'Even if such a fanciful notion was scientifically possible...' Dennis began.

'He didn't look at his phone while he was playing charades,' Jazz said.

'And according to dear Harold, his heart was fine,' Susan contributed.

'I was about to point that out, Susan,' Dennis said.

'I saved you the trouble, dear,' Susan said. 'You should be grateful.'

'On the other hand,' Jazz said slowly, scratching behind Pumpernickel's ears while she put her thoughts together, 'he might have known what was about to happen, mightn't he?'

'What do you mean?' Harold asked. 'Can I have just a tiny touch more of that cheese?'

He held out his plate. Jazz obliged him, not forgetting to drop a bit for the dog, who made a throaty noise of gratitude. 'The words he chose,' Jazz said. 'Dead Man Walking. Could he have been describing himself?'

'My granddaughter, Miss Marple!' Leo said admiringly. 'No wonder they gave you a scholarship!'

'It's an ingenious theory,' Dennis said, 'and it's good to know that the younger generation of your family has developed higher forms of ratiocination than your meagre mental resources permit. But if Harold is correct, and Julian's heart was sound...'

'Poison!' Jazz said suddenly. Pumpernickel barked. They all looked at him and Jazz.

'You agree with her, Pumps?' Leo asked.

'If we are now to listen to the views of a canine, however more intelligent he may be than his owner...'

'There are slow-acting ones, aren't there?' Marion said. 'Novichok, for one.'

'But as you pointed out, we all ate the same thing,' Leo said, 'and none of us have been affected.'

'Yet,' Dennis said darkly. Susan gave him a little nudge. Pumpernickel barked again, then wagged his tail.

'He thinks we're OK,' Leo said.

'Or he is demanding more cheese,' Dennis said. 'Too much will make him thirsty.' He drank half his glass in one swallow. 'I have every sympathy with his condition.'

'I'll open another bottle,' Leo said, getting up. 'Though Pumpy can smell poison. He has an extremely sensitive nose, and I'm sure he would have warned me when I was cooking...'

'He sniffed at Julian and barked, didn't he?' Jazz said. 'When he...like, didn't get up. If Pumps got a whiff of poison, wouldn't he have barked a warning if he thought it was anywhere else?'

'Then how, pray, was this noxious substance, if it exists, administered?' Dennis asked.

They all thought about this. Then Harold raised his head.

'Champagne truffles?' he said.

Leo sat back down. 'Did he get any?' he asked.

'He gets lots of things from his clients at Christmas,' Harold said. 'If you manage to find yourself a good builder, and Julian *was* a good builder, you'll do anything to keep hold of him, won't you? He was full of stories of how people throw themselves at him when he's bent over a breeze block showing his sunflower, and these were ladies as well as gentlemen...'

'Harold,' Marion said, 'try and answer Leo's question, there's a dear. Did he get truffles?'

'Yes, he did,' Harold said, 'and he kept them from me. He said I had more than enough presents, and they were bad for my cholesterol, though of course I'm on statins. He tried to make me mad by saying he could enjoy them because he did more exercise than I did, though I'm forever running up and down those stairs, seeing to all the little things that need to be just so if you're as fussy as I am about keeping your lodgers happy.'

'Granted that you are a fine physical specimen,' Dennis said, 'if you were aware of these chocolates, did you identify the donor? These are the questions to which my friends in the police service will demand answers.'

'He has a point,' Susan said. 'I don't know much about police interrogations – I glance at his columns, of course, but we're never allowed to watch crime series because Dennis says they're "complete fabrications", though if they asked him to write one, or even act as an adviser, he'd be on it like a shot.'

'I would not demean myself, Susan. I deal in facts.'

'And a fair amount of spicy speculation,' Leo said.

'I offer my audience the fruits of a conscientious investigation and share their natural curiosity as to motive. I may not be as skilled as the fair Marion in probing the mysteries of the human mind, but I would never stoop to the outrageous and ill-informed invention that characterizes the so-called dramas that flood our television schedules. I regard that as a dishonest and dishonourable way of filling the mouths of one's family.'

'We read a lot of crime at one of my book groups,' Susan said. 'It's the most popular genre after romance, and we like a bit of that too.'

'Isn't the point,' Jazz said, 'that if Harold can't answer a simple question about the truffles, they, the cops, might think he was guilty? I'm not saying he is, of course I'm not, because I think he's lovely, and would be happy to testify how much he loved Julian, and how shocked and grief-stricken he was over his death, just like all of us.'

There was a general murmur of agreement, in which Pumpernickel joined. 'And anyway,' Jazz continued, 'if they make any accusations, he'll have Gramps to defend him, won't he? So it's not as if he'll be carted off to jail.'

Dennis opened his mouth to disagree, but Susan nudged him, and he closed it around his glass, which he emptied, and cleared his throat meaningfully. Leo got up.

'I'm on my way,' he said. 'But of course my services are at Harold's disposal, should he need them. We'll all be subject to questioning, naturally, and all I would say is, just answer the questions they ask as honestly and directly as possible, without going off on digressions and distractions to which certain members of this company – no names, no pack drill – are occasionally prone.' He went out to fetch more wine before Dennis could respond.

'If he is referring to me...' Dennis began.

'You know he is, dear,' Susan said. 'Your digressions can go on for hours. They can be very entertaining, as well as educational, but sometimes they're exhausting. You're not going to change now, though, are you? If you did, I'd worry about you.' She patted him fondly.

'You don't seriously think they'll consider us as suspects, do you?' Harold asked nervously. 'I mean, how could they? All we were doing is playing charades!'

'They'll ask us all questions, sweetie,' Marion said. 'It's a suspicious death, after all, even if it turns out it was natural causes, which let's hope it was. And it's not a bad way to go, if that's any consolation. Peacefully and painlessly: that's what I'd like, a quick departure when the time comes, not stumble into a twilight that goes on forever.'

'I so agree with you, Marion,' Susan said. 'I sometimes fret, not about what might get me, whether it's cancer or dementia or some terminal disease, but about how Dennis would cope without me. Our children would be fine: they're all strong, spirited, independent people. But Dennis – he's a bit hopeless, though he hides it behind a barrage of bluster. He could never look after me if I got a lingering illness, so I want to spare him that. A quick exit, like poor Julian's: leave people with good memories of you, not of someone who didn't know what day it was, let alone that their skirt's caught up in their knickers showing they're wearing odd socks!'

Leo appeared with an open bottle of red wine in one hand, and a bottle of port in the other. 'I thought I heard sirens,' he said, 'but they went straight past. I guess trouble doesn't stop just because it's Christmas, or Chanukah, or any other festival meant to celebrate our survival.'

Harold blew his nose. 'I'm so sorry!' Leo said guiltily. 'Me and my big mouth!'

'It's alright,' Harold said, holding out his glass. 'I was thinking about what Susan just said. I could have looked after Julian if he needed constant care, but would he have looked after me? He was good at putting something right if it needed sawing or hammering or drilling or – don't get the wrong idea – screwing, but a sick body or a crumbling mind? Not so much. Maybe we should cover him up now?'

Marion rose from the table, picked up the sheet she had dropped behind her chair, shook it open, and flung it over the body. Leo put his bottles down on the table and helped her tuck Julian in. Dennis poured himself more wine.

'Contrary to what my dear wife says,' he rumbled, 'I am perfectly capable of looking after myself, and could also tender to her needs, should the necessity arise. A life devoted to exposing the crimes of our fellow humans might brutalize the sensibilities of other mortals – following the example of our host, I name no names – but it has not extinguished in me either the instinct to survive or the determination to fulfil the vows taken at our marriage ceremony. I am a very caring person.'

This was met with a silence broken by Pumpernickel giving a huge yawn.

'Pumpy!' Leo chided. 'Paw in front of jaw! Where are your manners?'

Harold tore his gaze away from the sheeted corpse and pushed his glass towards Dennis. 'Fill me up, then, there's a dear,' he said. 'As you're such a caring person. I didn't understand half of what you said, but I got that bit.'

'What he meant, in his roundabout way,' Leo said, not unkindly, 'was that he'd cope with the crap we all have to look forward to. Never mind the diseases, it's the little things that get you. Having to screw in hearing aids because everyone mumbles. Not being able to run for a bus. Forgetting, not just names, but the reason you were trying to remember them. Getting out of breath tying your shoelaces – not that Dennis has seen his laces in quite a while...'

'I have always favoured shoes I can slip into,' Dennis retorted. 'At least I have not sunk to wearing trainers in a ridiculous attempt to look young and trendy!'

'I wear trainers,' Jazz pointed out.

'You are young,' Dennis said, 'and for all I know you are also fashionable. You would surely agree that your grandfather is neither of those things.'

'Nor do I wear trainers,' Leo said. 'My father had very high standards in footwear, don't forget: he was a revolutionary in politics, but a conservative when it came to shoes. When my sister Becky swapped her shoes with a buckle for an American friend's basketball boots, he threatened to disinherit her. And though I still polish my brogues, I must admit I'm all in favour of Velcro strapping. In sober colours, of course: I think Dad would have approved.'

'Julian looked good in workman's boots,' Harold said. 'Especially when he wore shorts. He had good legs.'

'So do you, Harold,' Susan said. 'You haven't got veins or bulging calves: no need for you to struggle with surgical stockings!'

'Susan!' said Dennis, shocked. 'Such personal details, and around the festive board!'

'When one of the guests is lying there dead, there's no reason to mince our words, is there? That's one of the few advantages of dementia, as far as I can see. You can say what you like, and no one takes offence. Of course they don't know, any more than you do, if you're babbling or saying what you really mean, but it doesn't matter either way, does it?'

'Dennis rarely says what he means,' Leo commented. 'His writing can be very clear, but when he talks it can be like going into a cave full of cobwebs. Demented, though? I wouldn't call him that. He's not like my Deirdre. Or not yet.'

'I will take that,' Dennis said, 'as a compliment.'

'This seasonal harmony is all very well,' Jazz said, 'but we still don't know, because Harold hasn't said, who the truffles, if that's what killed Julian, came from.'

'To be fair to my little brother,' Marion said, 'he said he didn't know. And he's always been truthful, even when it got him into trouble. Haven't you, sweetie? Do you remember when someone – a grateful client – gave Dad a box of expensive liqueur chocolates, and you ate most of them? You put little stones in their wrappers, so the box still felt full, and it was only when Dad offered them to a guest that he found out what you'd done. He stopped your pocket money for a month, but it made Mum smile. Didn't she write you a note afterwards that said "Well done!"?'

'You made that up,' Harold said. 'I'd've remembered the note. She had very nice writing. Not like yours or mine.'

'But we went to boarding schools where they tried to force us to write italic,' Marion said. 'It was a craze at the time, like phonics was, until recently. We were issued with pens whose nib was cut at an angle, to make the difference between a thin vertical stroke and a thick horizontal one. We rebelled, of course, and as a result no one can read our handwriting except ourselves.'

'Isn't that true of all doctors?' Leo asked. 'Even the useful ones? I always thought it was to prevent outsiders reading their prescriptions.'

'This is all very interesting,' Jazz persisted, 'but surely Harold would have noticed if, among Julian's presents arranged around the Christmas tree – you do have a tree?' Harold nodded. 'Didn't you notice, then, if attached to all the beautifully wrapped gifts there was a label that could have come from a jealous lover? Or couldn't you read their writing either?'

Harold looked hurt. 'I hope you're not accusing me...' he began, but Leo interrupted.

'Of course she's not, Harold,' he said. 'She wants to find out what happened to Julian, like we all do. She's just a little impatient, that's all. She gets that from me.'

'Or possibly she's just the tiniest bit bored by all our reminiscences,' Marion said. 'This is the trouble with family Christmases: the stories come out with the paper hats and are as well received as the jokes in the crackers!'

'I'm not bored, or impatient, honestly!' Jazz said. 'And I'm certainly not accusing anyone of anything. But I do think it would be helpful if we could agree on a story to tell the police, when they eventually arrive. Otherwise we might be here all night, mightn't we, Dennis? You're the one with most experience of murder, if that's what it is.'

'Excuse me!' her grandfather said, raising his hand like a schoolboy in class. 'I know a bit about murder. I've defended several people accused of it, in my time, and one or two of them were found not guilty.'

'Which is hardly an impressive endorsement of your legal skills,' Dennis remarked.

'Of course I mainly deal with victims,' Leo continued. 'Those falsely accused, witnesses bullied by the police, the families of the deceased who were ignored or neglected...'

'That's all great, Gramps,' Jazz said, 'but what about Julian? If you were defending Harold, whether or not he's charged with anything, wouldn't the first thing you'd want to know be: what happened?'

Leo poured himself more wine, glanced at Harold, and raised his glass to him. 'Why should he know any more than the rest of us?' he said. 'I totally believe Harold's honest and truthful – we have Marion's word for that – and if he's in shock, like we all are, that's no reason to consider him guilty.'

'I have known cases,' Dennis said, 'where the chief suspect – not that I'm saying that is how Harold will be regarded – was traumatized by the sudden demise of his partner. An unexpected and apparently inexplicable event, in surroundings where criminality, let alone death, are the last things you would anticipate: could these not combine to warp and distort his memory and understanding? We are fortunate to be in the presence of someone who not only comprehends such events, but is practised in unravelling them.' He turned to Marion. 'Is my assumption sustainable or unwarrantable, fair lady? I bow to your superior knowledge.'

Marion pushed off her paper crown and ran a hand through her helmet of purple hair. 'Well,' she said. 'Of course trauma can affect the memory. But I've never analysed my friends or family, and I'm not going to start now. It isn't either helpful or professional.'

'You disappoint me,' Dennis said. 'In the absence of your expertise, we shall have to fall back on speculation, which by its very nature will be ill-informed.'

'Why don't you analyse those close to you, Marion?' Jazz asked. 'The rest of us do it all the time, don't we? Unless I'm very pissed, or stoned, I always ask myself why someone is behaving like an arse, or whatever. It's partly curiosity and partly self-preservation, isn't it?'

'Marion's always refused to analyse me,' Leo began.

Dennis, in between swallows, said, 'Because the sands of your mind are so shallow.'

'Because,' Leo said with dignity, 'she said it would change our relationship.'

'I wouldn't want her analysing me,' Harold said. 'She knows too much about me!'

'Isn't that the point?' Jazz asked.

'You can be too close to someone to see their virtues, never mind their faults,' Susan commented. 'Sometimes the more you know, the more you're put off.

Most people look better behind a veil, don't they? Certainly at our age!'

'You have no need of a veil, Susan,' Dennis said. 'The unvarnished truth...'

'Can be pretty ugly,' Susan interrupted. 'If you want to rub along with someone, you don't concentrate on their faults, do you? You prefer the nice things about them: that's only human!'

'I like to know the truth about people,' Jazz said stubbornly.

'That's because you're young, Jazz,' Susan said. 'When you've knocked about a bit, as we all have, you learn that no one, not even your grandfather, of whom I am very fond, is perfect. You have to learn to accept imperfection in the people you love, otherwise you'd go mad. Of course there are people whose imperfections make you decide you'll have nothing to do with them – politicians and other criminals, for instance – but if you like someone enough to take them on, you take on their faults as well as their good features. It's not a case of lowering your standards, it's just accepting that you can't change people: that's something they have to do for themselves. Isn't that how you felt about Julian, Harold? Or am I just being a silly old woman?' She took a sip of port while awaiting his reply.

'He wasn't perfect, that's for sure,' Harold said. 'But perfection's hard to love anyway. You might meet someone with a body like Michelangelo's *David*, but what would you talk to them about over breakfast?'

'I totally agree with Susan,' Marion said firmly. 'I'm a therapist, not an analyst, and all I do is what Jazz does, what anyone does in a caring relationship: help people talk about the things they find difficult, and shine a little light on them so they don't look so frightening. "The truth" can be very elusive, it's certainly very subjective, and a little of it goes a long way: it's like kryptonite, a small amount can be energizing, too much can be destructive. What most people want is reassurance that they're not alone, not the only people in the world to have suffered whatever they're going through. Of course everyone thinks they're unique and special, but when you realize that something you're ashamed of, and have been trying to keep secret, is in fact quite common, even ordinary, it often makes you feel better. Even though you still resist and resent the idea that you're not unique, and find it really hard to believe that anyone else understands exactly what you're going through.'

'OK,' Jazz said stubbornly, 'but how many people have been through what Harold's going through? We've all lost people we've loved and lived with, even me, but not to murder!'

Pumpernickel suddenly barked, which startled everyone as much as Jazz's words. 'It's alright, Pumps,' Leo said. 'Maybe that's the police. He's got very good hearing – certainly better than mine, which isn't saying much.'

'You are always interpreting his utterances in a way that confirms your beliefs,' Dennis said. 'I have long maintained he is more intelligent than you are, and I trust the arrival of the constabulary will decide whether a crime has been committed, or whether it is an unfortunate concatenation of circumstances.'

Harold looked distressed. 'What will they think of me?' he said. 'An old man with a beard and bracelet in a dress? Of course they'll think I did it!'

'First of all,' Leo said, 'we don't know it's murder, not before the pathologist has reported.'

'And not all members of the police service are as prejudiced as you appear to believe, Harold,' Dennis said. 'Transvestism is not unknown in their ranks, and those who choose it are not automatically regarded as criminal.'

'But you've got to admit,' Jazz said, 'that tolerance of people who are different is not their strong point. I understand why Harold's worried.'

'Of course he is,' Marion said, 'but he has nothing to be ashamed of, and certainly didn't do anything to cause Julian's death, which we all witnessed.'

'I hesitate to disagree with you,' Dennis said, 'but we merely witnessed that Harold made no visible move that might have caused the death of the unfortunate Julian. But until the cause has been established, that does not mean he is not implicated. It is not, in other words, an alibi that carries any weight.'

'They won't bring a pathologist with them, will they?' Jazz asked.

'On Christmas Day? Are you kidding?' Leo said. 'It'll be a couple of coppers who drew the short straw and who will take statements from us all when they'd rather be at home abusing their families.'

'Maybe Dennis knows someone who could clear things up quickly,' Susan suggested. 'He's always boasting of his contacts in Scotland Yard.'

'My contacts, Susan,' Dennis said grandly, 'are second to none. The commissioner will take a call from me as readily as the most lowly detective constable. But even I cannot conjure up a way of shortening a thorough investigation, which is the least we can and should expect in the case of our late friend. Given the time of year, and their shortage of manpower and resources...'

'People power,' Leo said.

'What?'

'You can't say "manpower". They have women too.'

'Is this an appropriate time for politically correct pedantry? There will be people in uniforms...'

'Unless you put in a call, dear,' Susan said.

'And who would I call, my dear Susan? The Home Secretary? Do I summon her from carving her turkey and stuffing, or, more likely, a nut loaf in thin gravy, to ask that she send someone to sort out an unfortunate death that, for all we know, may have been caused by indigestion?'

'You're always calling in favours, Dennis,' Leo said. 'At least, that's what you frequently tell me and Pumpy.'

'To shortcut a murder investigation, if that is what this is, would be as improper for me as it would be for Marion to analyse her brother, or you, for that matter! It would be unprofessional, and might actually do more harm than good. Questions would be asked, stories would be circulated, reputations endangered.'

'So you can't help poor Harold,' Jazz said, staring at Dennis with the same innocent blue-grey eyes as her grandfather. 'That's a shame. It'll all be down to Gramps, then, won't it?'

'What your grandfather usually does is muddy the waters,' Dennis said. 'I am of course willing to offer such assistance as may be within my power, but using my personal contacts in this instance will be entirely counter-productive. It is not that I am unwilling or unable to do so, merely that it will serve no purpose!'

'I think you've made yourself clear, dear,' Susan said. Dennis was about to expostulate further when there was a loud and insistent buzzing at the door of the flat that excited Pumpernickel into a frenzy of barking.

'That'll be the cops,' Leo said, getting up to let them in. Pumpernickel leapt up to accompany him. Everyone else, even Marion, who was usually so relaxed, sat rigid and expectant, not moving or drinking, hardly breathing. They heard the dog continue to make a noise, but whether it was a territorial bark or one of welcome was hard to tell.

~ ~ ~

'I don't want any more to do with them,' a female voice said as it approached the sitting room. 'Him I'd divorce if I knew a good lawyer, which rules you out, but you can't divorce your children, can you? I tried to leave them at home, but they stick to me like shit on a shoe.'

Pumpernickel bounded into the living room enthusiastically, as if to announce the new arrivals. A woman who looked very like Leo, only a bit younger and with a more bouffant hair style, appeared in the doorway.

'Happy Christmas, everyone!' she said. 'Sorry we're late, blame my useless husband, who just had to watch the end of some fucking football match that was taking place fuck knows where, and my equally useless youngest son, who chose today of all days to break up with his girlfriend, who was far too good for him anyway.'

She caught sight of the sheet-covered Julian, took a breath, and said, 'What, you haven't got round to opening all the presents yet? Or were you waiting for us and saving the best till last?'

'It's only my sister Becky,' Leo said, immediately behind her. 'This is Marion's brother Harold,' he continued, making introductions, 'and that on the floor is his partner Julian. Who is unfortunately dead.'

Becky took a step inside. Behind Leo, her husband Graham appeared with their son Jonathan. Graham was a wiry, balding man with a smile that was both cheery and resigned, as if he was trying to sell you something he knew you wouldn't buy. Jonathan was a good-looking youth with the slouch of an aggrieved adolescent. They peered over Becky's shoulder to gawp at the body.

'What, he died of your cooking?' Becky said. 'I'm not surprised: you use far too much salt.'

'Says the woman who thinks watching an egg timer is wasting four minutes of her life,' Leo said. 'We don't know what happened. We're waiting for the police.'

'Could be a long wait, I'm afraid,' Graham said. 'There's an incident in Regent Street. No one seems to know if it's a bomb or a gas leak. Everything's sealed off: the real reason we're late is we had to walk from Oxford Circus.'

'And Mum was on the phone to some actor in Poland,' Jonathan said. 'Hello, Jazz. How's it hanging?'

'Apart from a broken toe and someone who died after I guessed their charade, I'm great, thanks. Sorry about your girlfriend.'

'Yeah, well, Mum was keener on her than I was. She's into Shakespeare, and crap like that.'

'Forgive me, young man,' Dennis said, 'if, despite this being the season of goodwill, I take exception to your description of the greatest playwright the world has ever known as "crap". It is hardly an apt noun for plays that illuminate the human condition in words of such poetic majesty they are seared on the collective memory more than four centuries after they were written.'

'Except,' Becky said, 'they weren't all written by Shakespeare. No way, José. Hello, Susan. Still have the old ball and chain, then, just like me. Saints, we are. Why do we bother?'

'I'll get you all a glass,' Marion said, rising from her seat. 'And when you're ready, there's Christmas pudding and mince pies. Meanwhile, please help yourselves to Stilton.'

Becky took the chair next to Harold, where Julian had been. Graham sat by Dennis, Jonathan hovered around Jazz. Leo trotted after Marion; Pumpernickel looked round and decided to join the young people. Jazz was maybe a couple of years older than her cousin, but the dog could sense there was something between the two, even if it was only a shared sense of being injured. Like his owner, Pumpernickel was a romantic.

'You see?' Jazz said in a low voice. 'No one's taking it seriously.'

'On the contrary,' Susan said, leaning over to talk to her while Graham, an antiques dealer, discussed Marion's choice of paintings with Dennis while sizing him up as a potential customer. 'We're taking it so seriously,' Susan confided, 'that we can't really cope with it. We're all pretending to be brave for your sake – you know, the way a grown-up tries to show they're not afraid of snakes or spiders when a child's present. But we're all pretty shocked, even my husband. He writes about killings in gory detail, because that's what his readers like, but that hasn't prepared him, or any of us, for an actual death, here in this sitting room, amidst the debris of Leo's delicious pastry and the nonsense from those crackers.'

'Of course poor Harold's in shock,' Jazz said, 'but why do Gramps and I seem to be the only ones trying to pin down what happened?'

'Because you're a nosy parker?' Jonathan said.

'I am not!'

'Just like my mum. You've got the Wengrowski genes. I don't know whose I've got: Dad's only interested in flogging the crap he landed himself with because he's rubbish at auctions. I couldn't give a stuff about any of that.'

'So what do you care about? Not your girlfriend, obviously. No wonder you broke up with her!' Jazz said sarcastically.

'She was transphobic, if you really want to know.'

'Aunty Becky wouldn't stand for that. And she thought she was terrific!'

'Yeah, but Mum always assumes the people we bring home will agree with her on politics. She'll ask them about their background, and which playwrights they like, and what they want to do with their lives, but she never thinks we might – I might – be slipping someone past her who doesn't actually share her view of the world. She's all black and white, Mum; grey just isn't a colour she recognizes. She doesn't do shadows, or accept that some people live in them.'

'I know what you're saying, Jonathan,' Susan put in. 'When you live with someone with very strong views, who goes on about them loudly, you sometimes long for a bit of doubt and quiet, don't you? At my book club, I listen to people attacking and defending, and I usually end up siding with the people who aren't sure. We get criticized, of course we do, but just because people talk a lot doesn't mean they're convinced by what they're saying. They're often quite uncertain themselves, only they can't admit it.'

'Yeah, well,' Jazz said, 'you lot may be happy sitting around waiting for the cops to decide what happened, but I'm not. You any good with computers, Jonny?'

'Yeah. Why?'

'We could do a bit of digging.'

'You're asking me? After what you just said?'

'What did I say?'

'That I don't care about people!'

'I didn't say that. Did I say that, Susan?'

'Don't involve me, dear,' Susan said. 'I must say, I rather like this port. Why do we never have port at home, Dennis?' she asked, turning to rescue her husband from Graham's patter.

Jazz bent closer to Jonathan, while fondling Pumpernickel's ears. 'I was sympathizing with you,' she said.

'Funny way of showing it,' Jonathan said sulkily.

'Are you going to go on behaving like a teenage twat?' Jazz demanded. 'Or would you rather do something more interesting? Neither of us really wanted to be here, did we? I should be skiing, you should be, I don't know, feeling sorry for yourself because nobody loves you.'

'There are plenty of people who love me! And I'm not a teenager: I turned twenty in July!'

'Then you should try acting like a grown-up!'

'You can talk! You're only a year older than me, and I heard, we've all heard, what you get up to at *Oxford*. That doesn't sound very grown-up to me!'

'Don't believe everything you hear. Let's start again, shall we? See that body there, covered in a sheet that hasn't been properly ironed?'

'Mum wouldn't let that go. She's dippy about many things, but she's a fanatic with an iron.'

'Wouldn't it be fun to find out what they're not telling us, you and me?'

'How?' Jonathan said, in a tone that sounded intrigued as well as suspicious.

'We look things up. Follow a few links. We can use the spare bedroom.'

'What'll they think? Mum will say something about us slipping off for a quickie, you know what she's like.'

'I know. But do we care? It's better than sitting around listening to them droning on, isn't it?'

Jonathan was still doubtful. 'Just looking things up, that's all?' he said.

'What, you think I'm going to jump on you?' Jazz said, exasperated. 'I don't fancy you *that* much!'

'So you do fancy me a bit?'

'A bit, I suppose,' Jazz said grudgingly. 'I was impressed with your diving at the lido.'

'You're not a bad swimmer, either.'

'Thank you. So shall we slip away?' Pumpernickel raised his head. 'You can come too, Pumps,' Jazz added. 'Act as chaperone. Just don't tell anyone what we're up to, OK?'

The dog gave a grunt of agreement and followed them as they sneaked out.

~ ~ ~

'You are Romeo,' Becky said to Harold. She was a noted stage director, and she'd persuaded him – she could be very persuasive – to try a bit of drama therapy in Marion's consulting room while Marion and Leo were busy in the kitchen. She promised him it would help deal with his grief and distract him from worrying when the cops and the Christmas pudding would appear. It was better, she said, than sitting around drinking and listening to her husband and Dennis boring each other to death. Not that she minded people drinking, though she could feel mackerelled on a wine gum. It made her a cheap date, she said, but Harold could feel perfectly safe with her. Even though she wasn't sure about his taste in jewellery.

'This was a present from Julian!' Harold said, waggling his bracelet. 'And how can I be Romeo? He was a lusty young lover, I'm a bearded old queen!'

'It's not how you look, it's how you feel,' Becky insisted. 'You've just lost your best friend Mercutio, stabbed in a gang fight in a mindless act of violence. What's your first reaction?'

They faced each other, standing on the fitted carpet in front of the window which looked out on Hyde Park and the Bayswater Road, both fitfully illuminated in the darkness of a dull winter afternoon by the occasional car and the wobbling head-torch of a jogger working off, or working up to, his festive meal.

'Shock,' Harold said.

'OK. How does that express itself?'

'I don't know. There are moments I can't think about it, and moments when I can't think about anything else. So I'm kind of distracted and kind of numb.'

'Don't you want to scream? At the injustice of it, the senselessness and pointlessness of a life you cared about, a person you loved, being snuffed out?'

'I'm not much of a screamer,' Harold said. 'Sorry. I don't even scream when I see a mouse.'

'Don't be sorry. You don't even *want* to scream? You don't feel it building up inside, like water boiling in a kettle?'

Harold opened his mouth. A small burp came out. 'Sorry,' he said again.

'Enough with the "sorrys",' Becky said. 'The numbness is wearing off. Your closest friend is lying there dead. What do you feel?'

'Surprised,' Harold said. 'I can't quite believe it. I still can't.'

'What does your instinct tell you?'

'That the silly bugger died without telling me the passwords to his computer, so I won't know who to call. I think there's a sister somewhere...'

'Forget the sister,' Becky said. 'You can deal with all of that later. Concentrate on yourself for a moment. What do *you* need?'

Harold thought for a while. 'A cup of tea?' he suggested. 'Sorry.'

'Fuck the tea,' Becky said. 'Don't you feel angry?'

'Angry at who?'

'The world, for its indifference. Your friends and family, for not understanding your grief. The people who killed the man you loved most in the world.'

'Yes,' Harold said slowly. 'Yes, I see what you mean. I do feel a bit angry about that.'

'Good. Great. How will you express your anger?'

'The only time I get angry is if my bridge partner makes a really stupid bid because they weren't concentrating. I may go as far as an exasperated sigh,' Harold said.

'Stop thinking like Harold, Harold!' Becky said. 'You're Romeo, a man from a noble family in a small Italian town where gangs from rival families roam the streets looking for trouble. You're in love with someone everyone thinks is totally unsuitable, even your best friend, whose judgement you have always trusted. And now that friend is dead, and you think it may be your fault. You're not a man in a dress and court shoes, you're in a doublet and hose with a sword at your side. What are you going to do?'

Harold looked around wildly. 'I'm going to draw my sword!' he said.

'Yes!' Becky said She grabbed a pencil from a mug full of bits and bobs and thrust it into his hand. 'There's your sword. Now what?'

'I'm going to...wave it around,' Harold said. He swished the pencil in the air.

'And then?'

'I'm going to find the people who killed my friend...'

'They're all around you. Hiding in the shadows, waiting for you to make your move. Are you afraid?'

'A bit.'

'You're an expert swordsman.'

'I wish,' Harold said. He almost giggled, but suppressed it.

'You have been trained by the best. You are the son and heir on whom all the hopes of the Montagus rest. People look to you for a lead.'

Harold dropped his pencil arm. 'I wish they wouldn't,' he said.

'Why?'

'I don't like being the centre of attention.'

'Excuse me? You're a man who dresses in women's clothes and wears bracelets from a tart's boudoir, if you'll forgive the expression!'

'I thought you said I was in a doublet and hose?'

'Whatever. It's not an ordinary doublet, though. It's splashed with bright colours and studded with jewels like your bracelet. It draws the eyes of everyone who sees it. You dress extravagantly because of who you are. It's a deliberate choice: you can't avoid it. You don't want to avoid it.'

'That's not true,' Harold said. He put the pencil back in the mug and sank into the wingback chair Marion's clients used. 'I dress this way because I like the way the clothes make me feel. Other people think me odd, but I don't mind that. I'm more comfortable in a dress than I am in trousers, and I wear my dresses with pride, but actually I'm quite shy. People think of me as the bearded bloke in skirts and heels, and that gives me something to hide behind.' He shook his bracelet down. 'I don't always wear flashy stuff like this,' he added. 'I just thought it would suit this very special occasion.'

'What are you hiding from?' Becky asked. She tested the springs of the couch that was for patients who found it easier to talk lying down, and sat on it gingerly.

'Everything,' Harold said simply. 'I don't like reality much. I don't take on the problems of the world the way my sister does. I admire her for it.'

'Everyone does,' Becky said. 'She's far too good for my brother.'

'I like Leo. And he loves Marion. I like him for that.'

'Let's get back to you, shall we? The whole point of role playing is for you to release the inhibitions of your actual self and inhabit another character, such as Romeo.'

'I do that all the time,' Harold said. 'I've got no inhibitions about the way I look. The ladies I play bridge with accept me as one of them, only they shave more often than I do. The men, well, they either patronise me, which I ignore, or are hostile because I scare them, and there's nothing I can do about that, except try not to antagonize them.'

'Do they attack you?'

'They can see there's no point. I'm so inoffensive, it would give them no satisfaction.'

'What about Julian?'

'He's a builder in Brighton, he's used to oddities. He is – he was – rather proud of me, actually. It's as if he kept a couple of whippets, and suddenly he's got himself a borzoi. A borzoi who's not got a very big brain, who likes showing off, and is perfectly happy with his little routines.'

'But now he's dead.'

'Yes,' Harold said with a sad smile. 'Thank you for reminding me.'

'I'm trying to help you, Harold!'

'It's very kind of you, but I'm not sure I need it. There wasn't much help for Romeo, was there? Neither Juliet's nurse nor that doddering old priest could save him, could they?'

'I thought you were angry at Julian's death?' Becky said impatiently.

'Not really angry. More like puzzled. And sad, of course.'

Becky got up. 'Well,' she said, 'this hasn't had the effect I was expecting. Maybe I'm losing my touch.'

'What were you expecting?' Harold asked, standing and smoothing his skirt. 'Hysterics? Frothing at the mouth? Tears and tantrums? I'm really sorry to disappoint you.'

'Listen, you haven't disappointed me. I was hoping that by letting out your emotions you would feel better. But I'm not a therapist like Marion: I don't have the patience, never mind the training. I have a vision of people – well, of the roles I've given them – and I usually shout at them until they conform or convince me otherwise. But I deal with actors. They're not like normal human beings. Not like you at all.'

'You think I'm a normal human being?' Harold asked. He extended his hands, palms upwards, and shimmied a little to showcase his difference.

'You're probably the most normal person here,' Becky said. 'We'd better get back to the other crazies.' She took a couple of steps towards the door, then said, over her shoulder, 'Do you think Julian died a natural death?'

'I don't know,' Harold said, picking off a bit of fluff on his sleeve. 'I don't think so. He was perfectly fit, you see. All that manly exercise with bricks and concrete.'

Becky turned to look at him. 'You think someone might actually have killed him?' she asked.

'Put it this way,' Harold said, 'he may not have had Mercutio's gift of the gab, but he pissed a few people off. Maybe without meaning to, but it's the nature of his business, isn't it? Promising dreams that turn into nightmares.'

'My husband pisses me off without meaning to,' Becky said, marching towards the door, 'but is that enough to murder him? And on Christmas Day? That would be some present!'

~ ~ ~

'My sister means well,' Leo said, checking there was enough water in the saucepan over which he was steaming the Christmas pudding, 'but when she decides someone needs help, there's no stopping her.'

'If you mean Harold,' Marion said, rooting around in the cupboards, 'I'm less worried about what

Becky might say to him than I am over the fact that we haven't got ten small plates of the same set.'

'That sounds like something I'd worry about rather than you,' Leo said. 'Can't they use the same plates they've got for the cheese?'

'Sweet and savoury on the same platter?' Marion said. 'The nuns at my finishing school would be horrified! And I wanted to use the set Harold would remember from when we were young. To cheer him up, except I must have broken more than I thought.'

'You want to take him back to his childhood, when everything looked simple and secure?'

Marion stopped searching and looked at him. 'I suppose I do,' she said. 'How clever of you to notice!'

'I'm not just a pretty face,' Leo said, adding water to the saucepan. 'I should have put this in the microwave. Five minutes, instead of all this fiddling and faddling.'

'I guess I'm trying to pretend it hasn't happened. With Julian, I mean.'

'We all are, aren't we?' Leo said. 'Or we were, till Becky came. I suppose I should have put her off, really. But then I'd never hear the end of it.'

'I'm glad you didn't. She brings a bracing dose of reality to the proceedings. I'm going to take in whatever plates don't need washing to get rid of the spiders.'

'I do think Harold's coping very well. If something happened to you during a party, I don't know what I'd do. Probably go all to pieces.'

'No you wouldn't, sweetie,' Marion said. 'You'd organize everybody. You'd make lists. You'd ensure everyone had a job to do, as well as enough to eat and drink. Jazz is very like you, you know.'

'That's a good thing?'

'A very good thing. She's super bright. She guessed "Dead Man Walking" straight away, and that Julian was trying to tell us something.'

'You think he was?'

'Don't you?'

'Yes,' Leo said, 'but you're always telling me not to play the detective.'

'I think you're allowed, sweetie, while we're still waiting for the real thing.'

'I'm a bit disappointed in Dennis, to tell the truth. You'd have thought, with all his contacts, he'd jump in and take the lead.'

'Did you want him to?'

Leo rummaged in a drawer for a skewer to test if the pudding was done. 'I suppose I did, a bit,' he said. 'Which is sort of cowardly of me.'

'It's not cowardly at all. You've organized and cooked a magnificent meal for half a dozen people – ten, if you count your sister's family – and that's exhausting enough without adding in a sudden death. But you haven't let Dennis take charge: if he had, you would probably have resented it.'

'I would have grumbled, for sure,' Leo said, plunging the skewer into the pudding, 'but I suppose it would be a relief to be told what to do. Maybe old Dennis is losing his touch. Maybe nobody would take his calls, and he doesn't want us to know. Maybe he's almost as much of a victim as poor Julian. Except he's alive.' He pulled out the skewer and examined it critically. 'That's got to be done,' he said. 'It's been boiling for hours!'

'We should get back, I suppose,' Marion said. 'It's probably not good form to leave your guests alone with a corpse, though it's a situation finishing school never prepared me for.'

'It's shaken you too, hasn't it? Though you've put a brave face on it, as you always do.'

'I don't feel very brave,' Marion said. 'I suppose I'm just playing the role of big sister, as you're playing the big brother, but part of me would be very happy to give it up and let someone else cope.'

'I know exactly how you feel. If only we could get into bed and pull the duvet over our heads...'

'But we can't, sweetie. We have family to feed, as well as a possible murder to solve.'

'We could have a hug, though. Nobody's watching.'

'A hug would be very nice,' Marion said. Leo dropped the skewer and put his arms around her. She bent her head to nestle it between his cheek and his shoulder and gave him a long and loving squeeze.

They straightened up. Leo smoothed back his hair, checked his hearing aids hadn't come loose, and said, 'Should we light it at the table, or carry it in flaming? What do you think?'

'A flaming procession,' Marion said, 'would be a very fine thing, but we don't know if they're all in there, gathered expectantly. Let's wait till everyone's present, shall we?'

'You're so sensible. Which is another reason I love you.'

'It's a very boring reason.'

'Also because you're honest, and unafraid, and...and just beautiful, really.'

'Beautiful is going a bit far, sweetie. I'd settle for battered but mostly unbowed.'

~ ~ ~

'Do your folks boast about you to other people but rubbish you in person?' Jonathan asked, while tapping on his phone. He was sitting cross-legged on the carpet-like coverlet of the double bed in Marion's spare bedroom. Jazz was stretched out next to him, using one of the big pillows to cushion her head against the wall. The paper crown she'd got from her Christmas cracker was still in place, crookedly. Pumpernickel had squeezed himself between the two of them, and was apparently asleep.

'Don't everybody's?' Jazz said lazily, trying to see what was coming up on his screen. 'My dad doesn't say much, but Mum's always running me down for going to an elitist institution while saying casually, "You know she got a scholarship to Balliol, don't you? Thousands competed."'

'Did they?'

'Dunno. Does it matter? It's a lovely place, I'm having a great time, but it's not the real world, is it? You're more into that than I am.'

'Writing programmes for a crummy publisher of computer games? I don't think so!'

'You're earning a living.'

'I still live at home!'

'So do I. What's wrong with that? I'd rather put up with Mum nagging about never knowing where I've been than share a mould-infested bedroom with some girl who's either shagging or leaving half-eaten boxes of curry all over the place. At least I can rely on the washing machine and heating working, and the fridge being full!'

'Yeah, well, Mum encourages me to bring girls home, then she'll quiz them over breakfast about how good I was in bed. It's quite embarrassing.'

'Are you?'

'Embarrassed? Yeah!'

'Good in bed.'

Jonathan glanced up at her before returning to his screen. 'I've not had any complaints,' he said. 'How about you?'

'Me neither. But I get bored quite quickly.'

'Maybe you're not meeting the right people.'

'One thing about Oxford,' Jazz said, 'is there's no shortage of choice. It's just that they always want to talk about sex. Analyse it as if it was an essay question; why can't they just do it, and then get on with other things?'

'Maybe they care?'

'It's just like scratching an itch, except they can't stop scratching!'

'What if they care about you?'

'I care about them. I don't sleep with just anyone, you know! I'm very choosy, as a matter of fact. But it's not as if that gives them any rights over me, is it? Sex is like food: you take care to pick something you like, but that doesn't mean you want the same thing every night, does it?'

'I care about what people think,' Jonathan said.

'Of your performance? Or the situation in Gaza?'

'You sound like Mum.'

'I'll take that as a compliment.'

'Don't. She makes up her mind before she's talked to someone, and you can't change it. She doesn't listen, except to hear what she wants to hear. She doesn't ask questions, because she thinks she already knows the answers.'

'I listen,' Jazz said, 'but if I don't like what I hear, I move on. Like you and your transphobic girlfriend.'

'She wasn't really a girlfriend. We never slept together. Well, we did, once, but we never did anything, apart from talking and sleeping.'

'I think you probably have higher standards than I do,' Jazz said.

'I could lower mine a bit. We're agreeing on stuff, aren't we?'

'Are you coming onto me, Jonathan?'

'It's Christmas, isn't it? We're stuck here with our families.'

'And a dead body.'

'That's next door.'

'Pumpernickel wouldn't let us get too close.' The dog's ears twitched, but his eyes remained shut. 'And anyway,' Jazz said, 'you're supposed to be looking up stuff about Julian. What have you found?'

'Nothing much.' He tapped away, then stopped and stared at the screen. 'That can't be right,' he said.

'What?'

He showed her his phone. 'What am I looking at?' Jazz demanded. 'It's very small.'

'A marriage certificate?'

'Wait, Julian was married? But I thought...'

'So did I,' Jonathan said. He did some more tapping. 'Nadia Komoneva,' he read. His thumbs flew over the keyboard. 'She's quite pretty,' he said, 'if you like blonde Slavic types.'

'Do you? Because I'm neither.'

He glanced at her. 'No, you're not, are you?' he said, then returned to peering at his phone. 'There's a picture here of her with some Russian on a yacht.'

'Don't they all have yachts, the oligarchs? They try and outdo each other, like schoolboys and their willies.'

'This is in Brighton marina.'

Jazz heaved herself upright and winced because of her broken toe. Pumpernickel opened his eyes. 'Julian lived with Harold in Hove,' she said. 'They told me all about their house and their lodgers while Gramps was fussing over his vegetarian festive pie in the kitchen. I was a bit late, as usual, and he was worried about his pastry. But they were a couple, Harold and Julian, as much as Gramps and Marion or Dennis and Susan. I'm sure of that – and yet you're telling me he was married?'

'Unless there are two Julian Huskissons with their own building firms in the Brighton area.'

'The gold taps!' Jazz said. Pumpernickel shook himself awake.

'What about them?'

'He got them from some Russian he was doing work for!'

'Maybe they were a wedding present?' Jonathan suggested.

'Or they weren't good enough for this Nadia. But why would she marry Julian?'

'Maybe she was pregnant?'

'By Julian?'

'Or by the Russian.' Jonathan busied himself with his phone. 'She doesn't have a kid,' he said, eventually. 'Or not one she's registered, anyway.'

'I bet Harold doesn't know about this,' Jazz said. 'He's a bit like Gramps, he'll tell you everything, even if it's too much information, but he hasn't mentioned Julian being married. We can't tell him, though, can we?'

'Why not?'

'He's just lost his partner. Don't you think he's suffered enough?'

'You were the one who wanted to do a bit of digging,' Jonathan pointed out. 'Now we know, we can't unknow it, can we? What's the point, otherwise?'

'OK,' Jazz said slowly, 'but maybe it would be better if it didn't come from us.'

'What do you mean?' Jonathan objected. 'Because they think we're just kids? Because they believe all we do on our phones is watch porn and troll people? This is kosher material, I guarantee it, and I know what I'm doing. My mum thinks she's a computer genius because she can shop online, but she wouldn't have a clue where to find stuff like this!'

'Maybe we should get her to tell Harold.'

'Mum? She's about as delicate as a herd of stampeding buffalo!'

'Yeah, but she says what needs saying. She's well known for it, isn't she, Aunty Becky? If you want someone who'll tell the truth, however difficult or unpleasant, she's your go-to guy, right?'

'She has her actors in floods of tears, that's for sure,' Jonathan said. 'But they always come back for more.'

'Right, then!' Jazz said, manoeuvring herself off the bed. Pumpernickel jumped down after her, tail wagging, eager to help.

'That's it?' Jonathan said. 'I do all that work, and you're just going to hand it over to my mum, without even a thank you?'

'What did you expect, a quick fuck? We're first cousins, once removed!'

'So? We're not going to get married and have children, are we? You don't believe in commitment!'

'I've got a broken toe! And we can't do it with Pumpy here!'

'Who's he going to tell?'

'There's a long evening ahead, Jonathan, and the cops haven't even arrived yet. Let's just pace ourselves, shall we? We don't want to peak too early.'

'That's never been a problem,' Jonathan grumbled. Then he shrugged, closed down his phone, and got off the bed.

~ ~ ~

'It's not like you to object to a taste of luxury, Susan,' Dennis said expansively, playing with the glass Graham had just filled. 'I think it sounds rather splendid.'

Susan sipped her port. The three of them were the only ones at the table, everyone else being occupied elsewhere. Julian hadn't moved.

'I don't know,' Susan said. 'You know I get seasick on the Serpentine. That's why we never go on a cruise.'

'The boat's moored in the marina,' Graham said. 'It won't move any more than a ship in a bottle. I've had kids in wheelchairs coming aboard without any trouble.'

'And he's offering us a dinner cooked by a chef who worked at the Grand,' Dennis said. 'When the weather is more clement, of course. I can envision myself in a yachting cap and white flannels, gazing out to sea as the sun dapples the distant waves...'

'And the seagulls seize your chips,' Susan said. 'I'm sure it's all very lovely, and I know it's your pride and joy, Graham, but to be honest I don't like being on water, and Dennis is hardly built for boating, is he?'

'That is an outrageous slur, Susan!' Dennis said. 'I may not be the slender youth you married, but my size has never circumscribed my movements, and if I was called upon, say, to tiptoe through some tulips, I would do so with all the grace and delicacy for which I am justly renowned!'

'It's not as if you'd be racing at Cowes,' Graham said encouragingly. 'Nobody is going to yell at you to belay this or that: all they will do is ask softly if you'd like some more champagne.'

'Oh God!' Becky said, bursting in from the consulting room with Harold trailing behind. 'He's not trying to get you to buy his fucking boat, is he?'

Graham gave Dennis the rueful smile that conveyed complicity between husbands with strong-minded wives, and also showed how loving and tolerant they both were. 'Actually, Becks,' he said, 'I was offering them dinner aboard the *Hussy*. Dennis was looking for a birthday present for Susan, and I have one or two special things I keep aboard—'

'Crap you can't get rid of, you mean,' Becky cut in. 'Believe me, Susan, you wouldn't want any of that *drek*. No need to go all the way to Brighton: just come to my house, where you can't move for *forfalter* bits of this and that Graham was somehow persuaded was a bargain! Talking of which, where's the bag of presents I brought for Leo and everyone? I'm sure I put it down somewhere...'

She started looking around, but was interrupted by Jazz and Jonathan. Jazz said, 'Have you got a moment, Aunty Becky?'

'For you, darling? Any time!' Becky said. 'What have you and my no-good son been up to? If you've had a festive fuck I hope you're on the pill. I bet they don't include condoms in those Christmas crackers!'

'Mum!' Jonathan protested, at the same time as Graham said, 'Becky!'

'What?' Becky demanded. 'She's not such a bad-looking girl, even if there's a lot of Leo in her, and Jonny's just broken up with his girlfriend. You think they were practising their carol singing?'

Harold resumed his seat at the table. Graham automatically filled his glass, Susan smiled at him sympathetically. He avoided looking at Julian's body.

Dennis said, 'You are a denizen of Brighton, Harold. Would you recommend the marina as a suitable location for what was intended to be a surprise celebration of my beloved wife's birthday, were I able to overcome her reluctance to take to the water, and persuade her to accept Graham's generous invitation?'

Harold looked dazed. Susan leant over and patted his hand. 'Don't you worry, dear,' she said. 'The more he drinks, the worse it gets. Verbal diarrhoea, I call it, and there's no little pill to bung him up. Just nod or shake your head: it won't make any difference.'

'If you come into the hall for a minute, Aunty Becky,' Jazz said, 'there's something we want to show you.'

'Is it a present?' Becky asked. 'Because I've got one for you somewhere, only I can't remember where I put it. I didn't take the label off, or the price, in case you wanted to change it.'

'I knew this would be a waste of time,' Jonathan said to Jazz. 'We should talk to Marion.'

'You'd talk to her before your own mother?' Becky said. 'You got a problem, you come to me first. Are you gay?'

'No, Mum!' Jonathan said.

'If you are, it's something to be proud of!'

'I'm not gay, alright? It's nothing to do with me, as a matter of fact. We found something, that's all.'

'So now I'm a lost property office?' Becky said. 'What have you found?'

'We'd rather tell you in private,' Jazz said. 'Because...' She rolled her eyes significantly, taking in Harold and Julian.

'Ah,' Becky said, lowering her voice slightly. 'OK. Talking of gay...Come on, then.'

She led them into the hall and closed the door behind her, just as the door at the other end of the room opened and Marion appeared from the kitchen. She was carrying a pile of plates, on top of which she'd balanced a slightly tarnished silver dish heaped with mince pies.

Leo followed her, bearing a large Christmas pudding with a sprig of holly stuck in the top. He was singing, 'Happy birthday to you, happy birthday to you. Happy birthday, dear Jesus, happy birthday to you!' Pumpernickel, who had sneaked in with the young people, gambolled around his feet.

'I would have thought,' Dennis said, 'that a carol was more appropriate.'

'I was thinking of "Oh come, all ye faithful",' Leo said, putting the pudding down in front of his seat at the table, 'but we're not, are we? Faithful to one another, yes, but in the religious sense, no. Where's Becky and the kids?'

'They went out, looking furtive,' Dennis said. 'I trust they are not thinking of initiating another round of charades. The last one did not end well.'

'Don't be a party pooper, dear,' Susan said. 'Look at the trouble Leo and Marion have gone to!'

'They are generous hosts,' Dennis said, 'and I appreciate their hospitality as much as you do. Which is why I find it inexplicable that you should decline the invitation extended by our new friend Graham for an evening on his yacht.'

'Yacht?' Leo said, hunting in the drinks cupboard for a bottle of brandy. 'The way Becky talks about it, it's a clapped-out dinghy on which Graham spends more time and money than he does with his wife and children. He's been promising he'll sell it for a fortune since before Noah built his ark, but somehow the right buyer has never come along, has he, Graham?'

'That's not entirely true,' Graham said, his disarming smile intact. 'It's an antique sailing boat, and I've had several near-misses. I won't sell it to just anyone, you know: I've put in too much work over the years to give it away to someone who won't appreciate it. And it's certainly not clapped-out: I've restored it extensively, even extravagantly – I've an eye for detail, despite what Becky says. It's a thing of beauty, if I say so myself, and totally seaworthy. In fact I had an offer quite recently, which I turned down—'

'Because it didn't come anywhere near to covering the costs of what you've spent on it, according to my sister,' Leo said genially. 'Not that I'm taking sides, you understand. Ah, here we are. Finally!'

He emerged from the cupboard clutching a bottle of brandy. 'For the pudding!' he said. 'I should have made my own brandy butter for the mince pies, but you can buy it anywhere at this time of year, and it's one less thing to bother about.'

'You've done marvels, dear Leo,' Susan said. 'Your pie was so much more interesting than a dried-up turkey and watery Brussels. It was very kind of you to include us when all our children opted to go to their partners' families. Left to ourselves we'd've had a very dull day, wouldn't we, Dennis?'

'At least the only body would have been that of an unfortunate bird,' Dennis said.

'Kind of busman's holiday for you, isn't it?' Graham said brightly. 'Dealing with death?'

'Where are the emergency services?' Harold asked suddenly. 'It's been well over an hour! Does nothing work anymore?'

'It's alright, Harold,' Marion said. 'It's not as if they can do much for poor Julian. Have a mince pie. Do you remember these plates? I brought them from the house out of pure sentiment.' She handed him a pastry and pushed a plastic pot of brandy butter his way, accompanied by a tarnished silver spoon.

'Are these the ones we had in the nursery?' Harold asked. 'You used them when we had pretend dinner parties. You'd serve up something disgusting, like worms or frogspawn, and make me eat it!'

'Seriously?' Leo said. 'She forced you, my Marion? I don't believe it!'

'That's why Dad sent me to finishing school,' Marion said. 'He wanted to make a lady out of me. A total waste of time and money, I'm afraid.'

'They certainly didn't teach you how to cook,' Harold remarked, helping himself to brandy butter. 'You almost poisoned me, and how your son survived is something of a miracle. You were so lucky to find Leo!'

'I'm the lucky one,' Leo said. 'Before I met Marion, I was...'

'Insufferable,' Dennis interrupted, 'whereas now, thanks to her civilizing influence, you are...'

'A delightful host and an excellent cook,' Susan finished for him. 'And I think you've aged rather well, but then you always were rather dapper.'

'Dapper?' Dennis exclaimed. 'In those flowery shirts and ridiculous purple flares? He looked like a pimp clothed in cast-offs from Carnaby Street!'

Pumpernickel defended his master's taste with a loud bark that silenced the company. But not for long. Becky threw open the door to the hall and said, 'Harold, did you know Julian was married?'

Harold dropped the glass he'd been about to drink from. It fell onto the plate Marion had lovingly rescued, and broke it into several pieces.

'Married?' Harold gasped. 'That was something we were planning! The bigamous bitch!'

He got up, ripped the sheet from the body, and began kicking Julian with the point of his court shoes.

~ ~ ~

It took a while, and a good slug of brandy, to calm Harold down, and clear away the mess he'd made. Leo fussed over bits of china getting into the Christmas pudding, which remained unlit, but Becky told him to stop being such an old woman. Marion put her arm round her brother, drew him aside, and spoke to him softly. Pumpernickel sniffed at Julian until Susan shooed him away and diplomatically pulled the sheet back over the body to hide it from the averted eyes of the young people. Graham toyed with his glass of wine, his all-purpose smile intact. Dennis took over.

'Let us understand precisely what you have discovered,' he said to Jazz and Jonathan. 'There is no point in burdening the officers, when they arrive, with evidence that is speculative hearsay gleaned illegally from websites that exist purely to propagate nonsensical theories. How reliable are your sources?'

'I got him to do the digging,' Jazz said defensively. 'If he poked into places you're not supposed to go, it's my fault.'

'Your confession is commendable, Jasmine,' Dennis said grandly. 'It's a pity you have not learned to avoid emulating your grandfather, who is always overstepping the mark.'

'What she and young Jonathan have come up with is dynamite!' Leo said.

'If it is from sources deemed inadmissible, you ought to know, as someone who is still qualified to practice law – which is in itself surprising, given the dubiety of your methods...'

'Isn't it in the public interest, dear?' Susan said sweetly. 'That's what you always say, when someone threatens to sue you.'

'Of course it fucking is!' Becky said. 'It's tough poor Harold had to find out this way, but you can't hide from the facts my little boy discovered, and I'm proud of him!' She bit into a mince pie defiantly.

'Anyone can access the public records,' Jonathan said. 'I didn't do anything illegal. I could if I wanted to, but there was no need.'

'The ease with which people can access information that is supposed to be secure is an enduring scandal,' Dennis said.

'Come on, Dennis,' Leo said. 'You've had enough headlines out of material that was dubiously obtained! The big question is, what do we make of what the kids have uncovered? Julian was married to a girl called...'

'Nadia Komoneva,' Jazz supplied. 'And she was the girlfriend of...'

'Nikolai Mischkov,' Jonathan said, reading from his phone.

Graham's smile suddenly vanished. He picked up his glass of wine, but his hand trembled so much he spilt some on the table.

'What's up with you?' Becky said sharply. 'Look what you've done to Marion's cloth! Put some salt on it: it'll get rid of the stain. I warned you about having those beers while watching the fucking footy. Wine on beer makes you queer, isn't that what they say?'

'Never mind the cloth, Becky!' Leo said. 'Are you OK, Graham? You've gone a funny colour, and one corpse is more than enough!'

'What's wrong, Dad?' Jonathan asked anxiously. 'You're not having one of your funny turns, are you?'

'What funny turns?' Becky demanded. 'Your father's useless at telling jokes: he always forgets the punchline!'

'How would you know?' Jonathan retorted, looking concerned. 'You're always too busy with your actors to see what's going on!'

'How can you say such a thing?' Becky responded. 'I'm always there for you! Who does the washing and the cleaning and the ironing and the shopping? Cooking I'm not so keen on – I leave that to my brother, Bayswater's answer to Escoffier – but everything else...'

'Perhaps,' Dennis suggested, 'Graham would benefit from some of the brandy that proved efficacious with Harold.'

'It's only cooking brandy,' Leo said, grabbing the bottle from the many that littered the table, 'but if it helps...'

Graham held up a hand. 'I'm fine,' he said.

'Your countenance is still of a marked pallor,' Dennis said.

'He's always pale,' Becky said. She turned to her husband, determined to show her concern. 'Did you have a mince pie?' she asked. 'Actually, they're delicious.'

'I didn't make them,' Leo said.

'That's why,' Becky said.

Harold and Marion returned to the table. 'I do apologize,' Harold said. 'I don't know what came over me. The only thing I kick is a cupboard door Julian never got round to fixing. Must have been Becky's drama therapy.' He sat down with a brave smile.

'You listened to Becky?' Leo said. 'Are you crazy?'

'It was the shock of discovering that Julian was married,' Marion said.

'As always, you go straight to the heart of the matter, dear lady,' Dennis said. 'I have reported on many cases of bigamy in my time, and the emotional toll they take has frequently, I'm sorry to say, led to physical violence, and even murder, disguised as justifiable homicide, of course.'

This resulted in a shocked silence, which Graham broke by having hiccups. Jonathan poured some water into an empty glass. 'Here, Dad,' he said. 'Try drinking from the bottom side.'

'It never works,' Becky said.

'It's worth a try, isn't it?' Jonathan said defiantly. He put the glass in Graham's hand.

Graham took it and looked up at his son. 'That Russian,' he said between hiccups. 'You said Mischkov?'

'Mischkov?' Harold said, jerking his head up. 'That sounds familiar. Who mentioned him?'

'My son Jonathan!' Becky said proudly. 'You missed it because you were so overwrought.'

'Thanks to your therapy,' Leo muttered.

'Better out than in,' Becky retorted. 'As you always say when you fart. Marion would agree with me, wouldn't you, Marion?'

'About a fart, yes,' Marion said gravely. 'But I've never been a fan of letting everything hang out, I'm afraid. You can spend so much time tucking things back in, you miss the real point. What does the name mean to you, Harold?'

'I think,' Harold said, 'that's the name of the guy who gave Julian the gold taps. Though I could be wrong.'

Jonathan got out his phone, woke it up, and read from the screen, 'Nikolai Mischkov, Russian entrepreneur and former ally of Vladimir Putin. Charged with corruption, he fled to England, where he was granted asylum as an immigrant of high financial worth, and settled near Rottingdean, Sussex. A case of illegally trafficking people and gold and jewellery collapsed before it came to trial.' He closed his phone.

'And the Nadia Julian married is Nikolai's girlfriend,' Jazz said. 'There are loads of pictures of them together.'

'Now this,' Dennis said, refilling his glass, 'has the makings of a good story.'

'Shouldn't you wait, dear,' Susan said, 'at least until poor Julian has been removed?'

'Surely you know him better than that, Susan?' Leo said. 'He's like an old war horse: once he's got the scent of blood in his nostrils, you can't stop him charging!'

Jazz said, impatiently, 'Why would Julian marry a Russian girl if he's gay? And why would he choose to enact "Dead Man Walking" as his charade? What was he trying to tell us?'

'I don't know why people bother to get married at all,' Becky said. 'If you care about somebody, you don't need a certificate to prove it. If you don't, no certificate is going to hold you together. It's an outdated social habit, initiated by the patriarchy to take control of their wives' property.'

'Yeah, yeah,' Leo said, 'but it's a good excuse for a party. Deirdre and I celebrated for a week.'

'And look how that ended up!' Becky said.

'Susan and I,' Dennis said magisterially, 'have been married for forty-three years...'

'Forty-five, dear,' Susan said, 'and on our honeymoon in Scotland there was a drowning you thought was suspicious and spent three days drinking with the local police until they proved it was murder. That was your first exclusive.'

'You are definitely a saint, Susan,' Leo said.

'I know,' Susan said, 'but sainthood's quite boring.'

'Life with me is never boring, Susan!' Dennis exclaimed. 'If it was, you would be justified in abandoning me long before now!'

'I have thought of it, dear, many times. But the alternative might be even more boring. And I do have my book clubs.'

Leo poured her some more port, and said, 'I had a client who got married and divorced no fewer than seven times. He had no more faith in marriage than he did in the immigration policies of successive governments: he went through all that rigmarole as a protest, to give his various brides, all of them refugees, the benefits of citizenship. I managed to keep him out of jail for fraud, but only just.'

'That's it, Gramps!' Jazz said excitedly. 'What if Julian married Nadia so she could claim citizenship and live with old Nikolai, knowing she couldn't be deported?'

Graham shuddered. 'He's not so old,' he said.

'How would you know?' Becky asked. 'At least you've stopped hiccupping!'

'Becky,' Graham said, 'there's something I haven't told you.'

~ ~ ~

'That fucking boat!' Becky said, nursing a mug of tea Leo had made for her because she said if she had any more alcohol she'd murder her husband, and he wasn't worth spending Boxing Day in jail for. Everybody else, with the exception of Pumpernickel and the late Julian, helped themselves from the various bottles of wine and spirits that littered the table.

'Dad didn't know what it was being hired for,' Jonathan said reasonably.

'I am a little disappointed,' Dennis said, 'that what Graham described as a carefully restored jewel of maritime design turns out to be a tawdry vessel engaged in smuggling narcotics and young women destined for sexual slavery.'

'Did you ever see them, Dad?' Jonathan asked.

'What, you think he was invited to judge a "Miss Hussy" competition?' Becky said. 'This wasn't a game show, it was disgusting exploitation! I still can't understand how you were so stupid...'

'He was trying to hide it from you, Mum!' Jonathan said. 'He got into debt...'

'He's always in debt! He's so useless with money, they should make him Chancellor!'

'Come on, Becky,' Leo said. 'You have a nice house, your children aren't drug addicts, you terrify actors into adoring you, and you do a fair amount of what Dennis would call "unseemly scrabbling" to get the money to put on your productions. Your finances wouldn't bear inspection from His Majesty's Revenue and Customs either!'

'Do I get involved with gangsters?' Becky said.

'You would if you thought their cheques wouldn't bounce,' Leo retorted. 'Graham was only trying to protect you.'

'Protect me from knowing a boat he loves more than his family was never going to pay its way? I knew that already! How many times did I tell you to sell that thing?' she asked her husband.

'Many times,' Graham said, 'and I tried, even though I hated doing so. You could never see its beauty, the art that went into its lines, the glow of its woodwork when it was freshly varnished...'

'Please! Yacht porn I don't need! Show me one feature that compares to a single line of Shakespeare's for richness and beauty!'

'I appreciate Shakespeare,' Graham said. 'I just didn't want you worrying about a little hole in our finances when you were so busy trying to get funding for your *Hamlet*. But I couldn't sell a lovely old girl like the *Hussy* until she was as perfect as I could make her. And perfection costs money: you know that!'

Jazz said, 'He probably didn't know what Mr Mischkov wanted to hire the *Hussy* for, Aunty Becky.'

'He was too stupid to ask?'

'If you hire your car out, like an Uber, Becky,' Leo offered, 'you ask where the punter wants to go, not why. That's not your business.'

'It is if they use it for smuggling and murder! You're involved, aren't you? You're complicit!'

'I didn't know, Becky,' Graham said with a rueful smile. 'When I found out, I stopped him using it. Nikolai offered more. Enough to pay what I owed on repairs and finish the job. But still I resisted. I do have some scruples, you know. Even though Nikolai was seriously pissed off, I didn't say yes. I thought of another way of paying off the debts. Hiring it out for really swish dinner parties and such.'

'When you issued your invitation,' Dennis said sternly, 'I didn't realize you were intending to charge us for it. That entirely alters the nature of the occasion.'

'You're not prepared to pay for my birthday dinner, dear?' Susan asked mockingly. 'Isn't it lucky I said no!'

'I was not going to charge you,' Graham insisted. 'It was...a pilot scheme.'

'God spare us another of your fucking pilot schemes!' Becky said.

'Never mind the schemes,' Leo said. 'You might need a bit of protection against Mischkov, since you've refused his offer!'

'You mean, he might be poisoned too!' Harold said. 'Julian and Graham, they're much the same, willing to do anything for the thing they care about most. With Graham, it's his boat...'

'No,' Graham said, 'it's Becky. Always has been. And the kids, of course.'

'Funny way of showing it,' Becky growled. A fierce glance from Jonathan made her shrug and soften her expression from a scowl to a smile.

'I'd like to think,' Harold continued, picking up his glass, 'that Julian would say the same about me, if he was alive.' He held up the glass as a toast to Julian, and went on without pausing to drink. 'He took as much pride in the work he was doing for Mischkov as Graham is proud of his *Hussy*. But they had their arguments, Julian and Mischkov: I know that for a fact. You know when someone you love's upset, don't you, even if they won't talk about it. Maybe it was over this Nadia woman. Maybe it was because he was behind schedule and Mischkov got

122

impatient. Julian's not a thief, that's for sure, but he was such a perfectionist, and if he fell behind...'

'Like Dad,' Jonathan said proudly.

'If your father was such a perfectionist, why did he marry me?' Becky asked.

'Becky,' her brother said, 'shut the fuck up, for a change. Have another mince pie.'

'What if Mischkov paid Julian to marry Nadia?' Jazz said tentatively. 'To give her citizenship, obviously, knowing that she's not going to be tempted to sleep with her official husband? Who is someone Mischkov knows, employs and presumably trusts?'

'That makes perfect sense,' Marion said. 'Mr Mischkov can obviously be very persuasive, as Graham has shown.'

'Very,' Graham said, with a shudder. He drank more wine.

'Or,' Marion continued, 'Julian may have done it as a favour, to ensure he retained the building contract. Which, as Harold said, was very important to him.'

'So why would Mischkov kill him?' Becky asked. 'That's what you're all assuming, isn't it?'

'Maybe Julian threatened to expose something about him?' Leo suggested.

'He'd have to be very brave to do that,' Graham commented. 'Braver than me, I can tell you!'

'My hero!' Becky murmured, ironically. Graham smiled his resigned smile.

'He was brave,' Harold said, 'but I don't think he was *that* brave.'

'That voicemail on Julian's phone...' Jazz said.

'There was a message after he died?' Becky said. 'Don't tell me it was from the Other Side!'

'No, Becky,' Leo said, 'we don't know whether or not it was a pocket call, but we're pretty sure it was from Mischkov. Is it possible, Harold, that Julian was going over budget, as well as being behind schedule? If you're an irritable Russian gangster, these things can niggle at you!'

'*Niggle*, Gramps?' Jazz said. 'We're talking about a possible murder here!'

'What your grandfather means,' Dennis said, 'is that it is often a concatenation of petty incidents that can provoke an outburst of violence, rather than a single offence. And if this Mischkov, who I must admit sounds more intriguing the more I learn about him, is a man prone to violence, that means others who have fallen foul of him might also be in danger.'

'Do you mean my Graham?' Becky said. 'Is that who you're talking about?'

Dennis spread his podgy hands in a placatory gesture. 'I merely mention the possibility,' he said.

'It's his idea of being helpful,' Susan explained. 'I apologize on his behalf.'

Becky looked wildly around. 'You're saying we could be attacked at any moment? My husband could be taken from me, on Christmas fucking Day, surrounded by his loving family?'

'Becky,' Leo said, 'it may sound *meshugge* to say this to you, of all people, but don't be such a fucking drama queen. We're in a secure mansion block, though the porter's probably *shikker* on the sherry he's been given. Sitting round this table are enough sensible and able-bodied people to frighten off anyone with hostile intent, and we include the world's most fearless crime reporter –' he waved his hand in Dennis's direction, who acknowledged it with a modest bow of the head – 'and of course we have the world's most fearless guard dog!' Pumpernickel stood up, stretched luxuriously, then lay down again. 'Also,' Leo concluded, 'the police are on their way. So you can stop *kvetching*!'

'Except,' Jazz said, 'they got Julian. And he knew it was coming. We think.'

'That's just one interpretation,' Marion said. 'When you're in shock – and we all are, it's fair to say – you grasp at anything that will explain the situation. In the heat of the moment, and especially when you're full of booze, you can seize on something which, when you examine it rationally, doesn't actually bear scrutiny.'

'They were showing that movie, *Dead Man Walking*, on telly last week,' Harold said. 'He may have watched it, Julian, and it was all he could think of when it was his turn to do a charade. Which he didn't want to do in the first place, the poor lamb: that's why he disappeared to the loo. He was an artist when it came to architraves, but an actor? Even Becky couldn't turn him into Benedict

Cumberbatch. But I forced him, didn't I, and look what happened!' He drank his brandy.

'It's not your fault, Harold,' Marion said, patting his arm. 'Should we have the Christmas pud before it gets too cold to light? Once the police come, there's no knowing when we'll have another opportunity.'

'That sounds like a good idea,' Becky said, pushing back her chair, 'and I can give out the presents I *shlepped* all the way from Golders Green. Because my husband and my youngest son were too busy arguing over what was happening in Regent Street to carry a lousy shopping bag which I now can't remember where I put!'

'Actually, Mum,' Jonathan said, 'we were discussing the new England manager. And the bag had a picture of King Charles. I'm a republican.'

'Me too,' Becky said, getting up, 'but they were giving them away, and I have a soft spot for him, waiting so long for his mummy to die, and dreading it at the same time. I wouldn't want that to happen to you. You can shoot me if I go gaga. I give you permission, in front of witnesses including my brother the lawyer, though he'll probably charge me for adding it to my will.'

'Don't tempt me,' Jonathan muttered.

'It's OK, Becky,' Leo said cheerfully, pouring brandy over the pudding, 'I'll take what you owe me from your estate. Now, where did I put the matches?'

While Becky looked around half-heartedly for her bag of presents, Graham dug a plastic throwaway lighter from his pocket and offered it to Leo. Becky noticed.

'What, you're still smoking?' she asked. 'How many times have you promised to give up?'

'I have maybe four a day,' Graham said guiltily. 'It calms me down, a bit of weed.'

'It'll kill you, you know it will,' Becky said. 'If I don't do it first.'

'Have you really got some weed?' Susan asked Graham. 'I've never tried it, but I'm told it's very good for arthritis, and they charge a ridiculous price for those cannabis pills.'

'Susan,' Dennis said severely, 'you should not indulge in the use of illegal drugs, even in company as bohemian as this. Think of my reputation!'

'You've sucked on a joint or two at the parties Deirdre and I used to give,' Leo said, 'and don't say you never inhaled. I remember you and that girl – she'd been a Page Three model, in the days when baring your boobs was cool and cheered up the working man...'

'That,' Dennis said firmly, 'was a very long time ago. Unlike you, I have put aside childish things.'

'Those Page Three pics were nothing but exploitative bollocks,' Becky said, stepping over Julian's body to look behind the sofas. 'And since when were you a working man, brother dear? Ah, here we are.' She retrieved the bag from where she had dropped it when she first arrived.

Leo snorted and turned to light the brandy around the pudding. It took him four goes with Graham's lighter and resulted in a disappointingly brief flicker of blue and yellow. Everybody went 'Aaaah'.

Becky returned to the table with her presents. Pumpernickel padded up to her. He liked to know what was going on, partly because he was naturally inquisitive, partly because he regarded it as his duty as head of security, and partly because there might be something interesting for him. He'd received presents from everyone else, mainly squeaky toys that fell apart when you chewed them, and though he'd had plenty of scraps from the festive meal, and even consented to have a paper hat placed briefly on his head, he could still find room for a tasty little snack.

Becky dug into the bag and produced a wrapped present. Pumpernickel started barking.

~ ~ ~

'Should we call the bomb squad?' Jazz asked fearfully as they all sat round the table looking at the box of champagne truffles that was the first thing out of Becky's bag.

Graham rolled a joint with trembling fingers. He lit it, took a toke, then passed it to Susan, who looked at it, put it gingerly in her mouth, and inhaled. Holding her breath, she passed it to Jazz, who drew on it without hesitation before passing it to Jonathan. Susan exhaled, without coughing. She beamed. Dennis's eyes were on the truffles.

'There are no wires that I can see,' he said. 'The chances of an explosion are slight.'

'Maybe you should try a puff, dear,' Susan said, and giggled.

Dennis turned his gaze on her. 'When the police come,' he said, 'their view of what happened here will be coloured by the obvious presence of illegal substances. Should they regard that as grounds for arrest...'

'Come on, Dennis,' Leo said impatiently. 'They don't arrest you for possession, not on Christmas Day, and Graham hasn't got enough to be accused of dealing. Have you, Graham?'

'Not guilty, guv,' Graham said, trying to smile. 'That's the last of my stash. It's hard to get it over Christmas, you know? The strain of being cooped up with your family drives up demand.'

'Says my husband the drug addict,' Becky contributed. 'I don't mind the weed, it's the tobacco that kills you. No one's allowed to smoke in my house.'

'I've seen you having a puff in the garden, Mum,' Jonathan said. 'And then you talk to the rose bush.'

'At least it doesn't answer back!' Becky said. 'I need something to keep me sane, living with you lot, not to mention working with actors!'

'Cannabis damages the brain,' Dennis said. 'If you want an example, look at your brother!'

'There's nothing wrong with Leo's brain,' Marion said, smiling at her partner. 'I find it constantly surprising.'

'And there's nothing wrong with his body either,' Susan said. She giggled again.

Dennis frowned, but before he could say anything Harold asked, 'Why did Pumpy bark at the box? Where did you get it, Becky?'

Becky looked almost guilty. 'It was given to Graham,' she admitted. 'He doesn't like truffles, and nor do I, but I thought someone here might. People send him presents, usually the ones who want him to buy their old rubbish at an inflated price. I knew he wouldn't miss it.'

'So these aren't exactly new gifts,' Leo said, encouraged by the compliments paid by Marion and Susan. 'Not that I'm saying you're a cheapskate, but what would you call them? Recycled?'

'To be fair to Becky,' Graham said, 'I am offered any amount of tat around Christmas. I do a lot of business down at the marina, and there's a woman there, Hazel, I leave stuff with, and people leave stuff with her for me. She's very organized and reliable, a young widow...'

'Don't tell me she's one of those women with big knockers you yo-ho-ho with when you're not fiddling with your brass fittings!' Becky said sharply.

'Perhaps,' Marion said sweetly, 'Hazel might remember who left the champagne truffles for Graham? Unless there was a label on it that Becky removed?'

They all looked at Becky, who wriggled uncomfortably on her chair. 'I may have done,' she said. 'With all the *chazerai* going on, you expect me to remember everything? You think there was a little note saying "Happy Christmas, Graham. I hope this poisons you. Your friend Nikolai"?'

Dennis said, 'We do not, of course, know that these sweets are intended as an instrument of death.'

Leo stroked his dog's head, and said, 'I trust Pumpy. He's better than the best detective when it comes to sniffing out something wrong. He could smell what did for poor Julian, and he's identified the same substance in that box, I'd stake my reputation on it.'

'Scarcely an asset of high worth,' Dennis remarked, 'but even if we accept that the canine is correct, we need to identify the donor to establish that there is a connection between the demise of Julian and the intended demise of Graham. Otherwise the police, when they get here, will regard us, not as a party of respected and respectable persons whose theories are to be taken seriously, but as a collection of stoned inebriates who should probably be locked up to ensure the safety of the public. If, of course, there were any cells vacant.'

'We know,' Jazz said, idly crumbling bits of Stilton, which attracted Pumpernickel to sit expectantly at her feet, 'that Nikolai Mischkov used both Julian and Uncle Graham to get what he wanted. Harold said Julian was falling behind schedule, and he may, or may not, have known what the penalty for that was. Whoever made that call mentioned someone being dead: maybe that was Julian? Did everyone in your circle, Harold, know you and Julian were coming here for Christmas?'

'I made no secret of it,' Harold said. 'We received loads of invitations, but I told everyone we were going to my big sister's. And we were going to announce our intention to marry!'

Marion silently handed him a tissue. He blew his nose loudly.

'Does everyone in Brighton and Hove know Marion and Gramps are an item?' Jazz persisted. She flicked the dog a little ball of cheese, which disappeared before it hit the ground.

'We've been together for more than five years,' Leo said. 'It's common knowledge. Why are you asking?'

'Because, Gramps,' Jazz said, 'what if you were the link? If Uncle Graham is also a target, and he's married to your sister, who usually celebrates Christmas with you...'

'Not *every* Christmas,' Becky said. 'We're not that desperate.'

'Come on, Mum,' Jonathan said. 'I've never known a Christmas when Uncle Leo wasn't around.'

'We're family!' Becky said. 'You can't escape it, you might as well embrace it!'

'Do you really think Leo is the target, Jazz?' Susan asked. 'I suppose, as a successful lawyer, he must have made lots of enemies.'

'That depends, my dear Susan,' Dennis said, refilling his glass, 'on your definition of success.'

'Surely Uncle Graham is a target,' Jazz said, 'but maybe we all are! Maybe this Mischkov has spies everywhere and is planning to get rid of us all!'

'If you are including me in your fantastical hypothesis,' Dennis said, 'I have in the past been the object of an oligarch's ire, but that particular individual has long since died – poisoned, as a matter of fact, by a jilted lover – and I cannot imagine why I should be targeted by another such miscreant. I haven't written about any Russians for more than a year, and though they are known to nurture grudges for an inordinate length of time, I cannot think of anyone who might want to be rid of me. I may arouse the hostility of certain criminals whose activities I expose, but as far as I'm aware I have never written anything that could enrage Mr Mischkov.'

'Perhaps what he wants, dear,' Susan said, 'is for you to be a witness to his cunning plan, and write about how clever he is. To be the centre of a story by the world's most fearless crime reporter: that's a sort of celebrity, isn't it?'

'I suppose that's possible,' Dennis said complacently, ignoring the irony in Susan's tone. 'It seems, however, unlikely that this whole charade was staged for my benefit. And how would he know I was here? Our social arrangements scarcely rate a mention in what used to be called the court pages, but have become tittle-tattle related by semi-literate television personalities.'

Marion picked up a slightly tarnished silver cake-slice. 'I'm going to have some Christmas pudding,' she announced. 'Leo's been boiling it for hours, and it would be a pity to let it go to waste. Does anyone else want some?'

She was about to plunge in the cake-slice when there was a prolonged buzzing at the front door. Pumpernickel naturally barked. Marion said, 'That, surely, must be the emergency services. Now we'll never get to the pudding!'

'I'll go,' Leo said. 'You carry on carving.' He and the dog left. Dennis held out his plate.

'I would like a small portion, dear lady,' he said. 'I rarely take dessert, but with all the distractions this day has provided, the comfort of traditional sustenance would be quite welcome. Especially when accompanied by brandy butter.'

~ ~ ~

'Mr Arbuthnot!' said the elderly uniformed sergeant on being ushered into the room by Leo. 'Happy Christmas! I haven't seen you since you drank "Knobber" Keys under the table, making it nice and easy for us to charge him with the Pinner murders. What a story that made, eh? How the devil are you?'

Dennis paused in the act of spooning brandy butter over his pudding. 'Sergeant Barron,' he acknowledged, coolly. 'I thought you'd retired.'

'Soon, Dennis, soon. Easter, as a matter of fact. Can't wait. Hello, folks!' he said cheerily to everyone round the table. 'I'm Sergeant Arthur Barron. Known old Dennis here since he was a stick-thin reporter for the *News of the Screws*. Used to enjoy those raids on the brothels in Balham, didn't we? What's the story here, then?'

Susan giggled, Dennis looked affronted. Leo said, 'I don't suppose you can have a drink on duty, sergeant, even though it's Christmas. Would you like a tea, or coffee?'

'Or some Christmas pudding?' Marion offered. 'I'm Marion Fitzwalter, this is my flat—'

'Marion Fitzwalter, the shrink?' Arthur asked. 'I've heard of you. A legend, you are. When colleagues fall apart, you put their heads together! It's an honour to meet you, ma'am!' He held out his hand, which Marion, after putting down the cake-slice, shook heartily.

'This is my brother Harold,' Marion said. 'It's his partner lying there under the sheet.'

Arthur looked Harold up and down. 'I don't judge,' he said, 'but I bet you didn't get that dress from Evans, did you?'

'Shein, as a matter of fact,' Harold said. 'I don't normally shop online, but...'

'You want to try before you buy, don't you? Then you don't have to go through all that rigmarole of returning it at the post office. If you can find one that's open.'

'Arthur,' Dennis said, 'where are your colleagues? We have at the very least a suspicious death, and need a pathologist, or at any rate a medical examiner, before the body can be removed.'

Arthur lifted the sheet, looked at Julian's body, then let the sheet drop again. 'He's not going anywhere, is he?' he said. 'He's hardly started to smell. And you've very sensibly got on with your dinner.' He sniffed the air. 'As well as smoking the whacky baccy,' he added. 'I won't dwell on that, as you're friends of Dennis's, and he wouldn't be caught breaking the law, would he?' He gave a ferocious wink and made a nudging gesture with his elbow. 'I'm not asking for sympathy, but I've been on duty since six, and all I've had is an out-of-date Cornish pasty. Which was cold.'

'Would you like a plate of food?' Leo offered. 'There's plenty left, as you can see.'

Arthur looked at the debris on the table and shook his head. 'I'm very tempted,' he said, 'especially as I see you've done without a turkey – one of the most boring birds in the world, and one of the ugliest, if you ask me – but I'd better not. I'm supposed to be losing weight, but at my age, what's the point? I'm not as big as old Dennis here, but they still mutter about me passing the fitness test. Can you imagine me running a marathon? That's what my guv'nor hinted at. For charity, if you please! Charity begins at home, I told him – and since we're on the subject, maybe I will have a bit of that pudding, ma'am, if it's going. I've got a weakness for sweet things, like my old mucker Dennis, and it is Christmas, after all.'

Dennis was about to protest, but an amused look from his wife made him concentrate on the brandy butter, of which he took another generous spoonful before pushing it towards the sergeant.

'I thank yew,' Arthur said, taking the plate Marion offered him and adding a dollop of brandy butter. 'That was Arthur Askey's catchphrase: my old man was so keen on him, he named me after him. But,' he said, turning to Jazz and Jonathan, 'I bet you young people have never heard of him, have you? Little chap, he was, with big glasses. A great comedian. Tell me what you think happened here.'

He ate a spoonful of pudding while waiting for them to answer. Jonathan said, 'I wasn't here when it happened. I only arrived after, with my mum and dad.'

'But,' Jazz said, 'he discovered things we didn't know. I was present when Julian died. I guessed his charade was "Dead Man Walking": he just lay down and didn't get up. One minute he was acting, the next he was dead.'

'Sounds like a heart attack to me,' Arthur said. 'That would make it nice and easy for all of us, wouldn't it? Best Christmas present you could ask for – except for the deceased, of course.'

Harold said, 'He was perfectly healthy, unless he was hiding something from me. But why would he? We were going to get married!'

'Congratulations,' Arthur said, 'and commiserations too. What did you discover, young man?'

'His name's Jonathan,' Becky said, 'and don't you start harassing him. I know what you're like!'

'Do you, madam? I'll do my best to live down to your expectations. So, Jonathan. I promise I won't beat you up, not in front of witnesses. What did you find?'

'Julian was married,' Jonathan said. 'To a woman called Nadia Komoneva.'

'Was he now?' Arthur turned to Harold. 'That must have been a bit of a surprise.'

'You can say that again,' Harold affirmed. 'We don't go in much for bigamy, even in Brighton and Hove.'

'Is that where you are? I was thinking of retiring there, though I probably couldn't afford it.'

'Harold runs a boarding house,' Leo said helpfully. 'I'm sure he could...' Pumpernickel stopped him going further with a warning yap. 'Sorry, yes,' Leo said. 'It's the romantic in me.'

'Does you credit, sir,' Arthur said. He wiped his fingers on his trousers and got out his phone. 'We could all do with a bit more romance in our lives, couldn't we? Ask old Dennis!'

'Sergeant!' Dennis said sharply. 'I know we go back a long way, but this is hardly the time...'

'Sorry, Dennis,' Arthur said, glancing up from his phone and taking in Susan. 'Is this your good lady? Very nice to make your acquaintance, ma'am. You've got a solid one there!'

'I know, sergeant,' Susan said, smiling. 'Though we've been together for a *very* long time, I'm learning new things about him all the time.'

'I could tell you some stories, ma'am,' Arthur said, while engrossed in his phone. 'I won't forget Marilyn, as long as I live.'

Dennis started to protest, but Susan said, quickly, 'Who was Marilyn, sergeant? Don't keep us in suspense!'

'Nobody, Susan,' Dennis said severely. 'Sergeant Barron has better and more important things to do than rake up frivolous memories of youthful incidents. May I remind you that we are material witnesses in an investigation...'

'Youthful follies?' Susan said. 'Tell me more! Did you know about Marilyn, Leo?'

Leo shook his head. 'Doesn't ring a bell,' he said, 'but then my memory card is pretty full. It's what happens at our age, isn't it? I can remember being surrounded by beautiful people, not to mention the booze and the other substances that usually circulated, but the only Marilyn I can think of is Monroe!'

'You're protecting him, aren't you?' Susan said. 'Of course you would, even though it's more than he deserves. But I'd still like to know. Marion would agree that a painful truth is better lanced than allowed to suppurate.'

'Susan!' Dennis said. 'You are, to employ a tedious cliché, making a mountain out of a molehill. I can assure you that Marilyn...'

Arthur looked up from his phone. 'Marengo,' he said. 'That was her name. Not Monroe, Marengo. Probably not her real name, but anyway. Very pretty girl. An art student, long blonde hair, wearing one of those skimpy dresses that leave nothing to the imagination. Protesting, she was. I can't remember what she was protesting about...'

'The poll tax,' Dennis said. 'One of the stupidest ideas Thatcher ever had. Why should the Duke of Westminster pay the same community charge as an art student in a basement?'

'There were riots,' Leo said. 'I took part, though I never got arrested.'

'You never did,' Dennis said sourly.

'Marilyn wasn't arrested, but her boyfriend was,' Arthur said. 'Beaten up quite badly, he was – not by me, I hasten to add. She made her own protest, outside Savile Row cop shop, wasn't it, Dennis? Long since closed, of course. Very fine building.'

'Are you going to tell us what the fuck happened, sergeant?' Becky exploded. 'Or are you going to give us a lecture on police architecture?'

'Marilyn Marengo set herself on fire on the pavement, madam. And Mr Arbuthnot, who'd been asking questions about injured coppers, took off his jacket and smothered the flames with it. He saved Marilyn's life, not that she was grateful.' He returned to his phone.

Susan said to her husband, 'Did I know you then?'

'I had seen you, Susan,' Dennis said, 'but you didn't notice me. I was a junior reporter, and I ruined a perfectly good suit. My only suit, as a matter of fact.

Though the paper recompensed me in return for the story.'

'You never told me about this,' Leo said.

'It was nothing to boast of. You and I held different views. I wouldn't want you to think I was a convert to whichever cause you were supporting that week.'

'Write a book, I could, if I had the time,' Arthur remarked, oblivious to the atmosphere he had created. 'Maybe I'll have a go, when I retire.'

'I look forward to reading it,' Susan said. 'I could recommend it to one of my book clubs. We like something sensational, especially at Christmas.'

'One of our busiest times, Christmas,' Arthur said, still tapping at his screen with one hand while spooning pudding into his mouth with the other. 'You're not the only ones sitting around a dead body, I can tell you that. Out there, everything's going to pot!'

'Can I ask what's happening in Regent Street, sergeant?' Graham said diffidently. 'Our Uber was stopped and we had to walk!'

'That's another thing you can blame on the government, sir,' Arthur said, who could talk, chew and concentrate on his screen all at the same time. 'You know that security minister they fired? He went bananas – Christmas Day brings out the worst in people who are already under strain – and tried to blow up the Cafe Royal. The device didn't go off – he'd been in charge of MI5, what do you expect? – but obviously we have to take it seriously. Ah, here we are. Nadia Komoneva. Kept her maiden name, I notice. She's dead too, I'm afraid.'

He finished his pudding amid a silence Harold was the first to break. 'How?' he croaked.

Pumpernickel barked. Leo said, 'Poison, you want to bet?'

'Almost right, sir,' Arthur said, 'though I'm afraid you don't get a cigar. No one smokes them these days, do they, though they don't mess with your brain the way weed does. Why do you think it was poison, Mr Wengrowski?'

'We have not been sitting here idly awaiting your arrival,' Dennis said magisterially. 'There are some great minds gathered around this table, Sergeant Barron, and though we have toyed with, and dismissed, a great deal of extravagant speculation...'

'The dog knew the answer,' Leo said, patting Pumpernickel fondly.

'Thank God he can't talk,' Becky said, 'or we'd have to listen to even more bollocks than we have already. That pudding's good, though. So who killed Nadia whatever-her-name-is?'

'My guess would be...' Dennis began, but Jazz interrupted.

'Nikolai Mischkov?' she said.

'Bang on, young lady!' Arthur said. 'Have you ever thought of joining the police service?'

'My niece, a pig?' Becky said. 'Over my dead body!'

'She's your great-niece, Becky,' Graham said, 'and my guess is that she'll do exactly what she wants. Like our own children, and they haven't done so badly, have they?'

'Has Mr Mischkov been arrested?' Marion asked.

'He has indeed, ma'am,' Arthur said. 'My colleagues in the Sussex police have charged him with murder. They found poisonous materials...'

'Which Pumpy identified!' Leo said.

'And my Graham could have been next!' Becky said. She pushed the box of champagne truffles towards Arthur.

'I thank yew!' Arthur said. He opened the box and popped a truffle into his mouth before anyone could stop him. 'What?' he said, after swallowing. 'They're delicious!'

'Some of us,' Dennis said, eyeing Arthur, like everyone else, with that mixture of fascination and horror that accompanies the expectation of imminent death, 'were ready to believe those were a gift from Mr Mischkov intended to despatch our friend here, the motive being a dispute over the use of an antique boat called the *Hussy* that might generously be described as a yacht.'

'Julian was sent a box just like it,' Harold said. 'One of the many presents we opened just before coming here. We think, though we don't know yet, that's what killed him. Maybe you should make yourself sick?'

'I feel fine!' Arthur said.

'So did Julian,' Harold said, 'until after the roasted Brussels.'

'Cooked by my brother,' Becky said. 'They always give me wind.'

'Julian,' Harold said, 'was behind schedule with Mischkov's building work, and may have been over budget too. Even if he really did marry that girl to enable her to stay in this country...'

'Don't forget the voicemail,' Jazz said. She turned to Arthur. 'Shouldn't you ask for an ambulance or something?'

'Don't worry about me, miss,' Arthur said. 'Forty years as a copper gives you the constitution of a rhino. And Nadia Komoneva was battered to death with an antique brass lamp in the art nouveau style, according to these notes.'

'Sounds like one of a set I sold him!' Graham said.

'Does that make him an accomplice?' Becky asked Leo.

'No way!' her brother said.

'You'd better be right,' Becky said. 'We're giving a New Year's Eve party, and he's in charge of the punch. You're invited, by the way.'

'Have the poisons been identified?' Marion enquired.

Arthur consulted his phone. 'Not definitively,' he said. 'Speculation is they're the kind used to nobble racehorses. Mr Mischkov has quite a stable, apparently.'

'What about this?' Jazz said. She picked up Julian's phone from the table and replayed the voicemail they'd all heard. They waited for Arthur's reaction.

'Well, miss,' he said, pushing aside his now empty plate, 'that confirms what my West Sussex colleagues witnessed when they arrived. Mr Mischkov and his girlfriend had an argument. According to Mr Mischkov, it was over a bracelet he had given to somebody for safekeeping. The girlfriend accused him of promising the bracelet to her, then breaking his promise. He swore he'd been trying to get it back, but she didn't believe him. She attacked him, and he hit her with the first thing that came to hand. He insists he didn't mean to kill her. He boasted, in a somewhat drunken way, of killing the person who had failed to return the bracelet, and that he would kill everyone who kept it from him. It is, apparently, a priceless heirloom given by some tsar or other to Mr Mischkov's family.'

Harold unconsciously jingled his bracelet down his wrist. Everyone stared at it. Pumpernickel let out a low growl.

'What?' Harold said, holding the bracelet up. 'You don't think...?'

'Where did you get that, sir?' Arthur asked.

'From Julian!' Harold said. 'A little Christmas present. It's only costume jewellery.'

Graham said, quietly, 'It looks real enough to me, Harold.'

'Like you'd know!' Becky scoffed.

'He would, Mum!' Jonathan insisted. Becky shrugged.

Arthur was tapping his phone again. 'Can I have a look at it?' he said. Harold unclipped it and handed it to him. 'Diamonds, emeralds and rubies,' Arthur read from his screen. 'We'll have to keep this, I'm afraid, for expert examination.'

'You mean, it might be real?' Harold said.

'If it is, it's probably worth a quarter of a million,' Graham said.

Harold put his hands to his mouth. 'I thought it was paste!' he said. 'And I got him a pair of cowboy boots from one of those pre-loved sites!'

'If this bracelet is genuine,' Dennis said, 'are you, or your West Sussex colleagues, Arthur, suggesting that Julian was the person to whom Mr Mischkov gave it for safekeeping, and he then refused to return it?'

'Julian would never steal!' Harold maintained. 'Certainly not something that valuable!'

'What if Mischkov gave it to him to keep it out of Nadia's hands?' Leo suggested. 'And Nadia nagged him into changing his mind, so he demanded it back. Maybe Julian wanted to keep hold of the bracelet till he had finished work on the mansion. You know, as security against payment. Maybe that's why Mischkov killed him.'

'He said it was a present,' Harold wailed. 'He gave me stolen goods! I'll be next in the firing line!'

'No, Harold,' Marion said firmly. 'He sacrificed himself for you. You found the bracelet by accident, you liked it, Julian didn't want to disappoint you, so he made you a present of it. He knew what was likely to happen. Maybe he even tipped off the police.'

'They did receive a warning, ma'am,' Arthur said, 'but they were a little late acting on it. It is Christmas Day, after all! But I'll make sure you're safe, Mr Fitzgerald. You have my word on it.'

'Please call me Harold,' Harold said gratefully.

'What about my Graham?' Becky said.

'I don't think he's in any immediate danger, madam,' Arthur said. 'Not now Mr Mischkov is in custody.'

'Well,' Becky said, punching her husband on the shoulder, 'maybe you got yourself on a hit list! *Mazel tov!*'

'Julian was obviously a very caring and very generous man,' Marion said.

'He never told me about his marriage, though,' Harold said, sniffing.

'Maybe he would have,' Leo said, 'only the poison acted quicker than he anticipated.'

'If it was poison,' Dennis said. 'We still await expert confirmation. Whatever the case, it appears that he was a victim of someone whose thirst for revenge will never be sated.'

'Fortunately,' Arthur said, 'we caught him before he can do any more damage. And though you've lost the person you loved, Harold, you've got to admit it's not a bad way to go. I'd rather that than dribble my life away waiting for the carers to change my nappy, wouldn't you? Enjoy what you've got while you can, I say.'

'I agree with you,' Harold said. 'Can I try one of those truffles?'

'Despite Pumpernickel's warning?' Leo said. 'Is that wise?'

'He's a wonderful dog,' Marion said. 'Aren't you, Pumps?' The dog responded by bounding over to her and lying on his back to have his tummy scratched. Marion obliged, while continuing, 'But he may not be right every time. I'm not, Leo's not, even Dennis has been known to get things wrong, but do we love them any the less? Of course not!'

'Being right all the time is so boring!' Susan said.

'I shall endeavour to avoid boring you in future, Susan,' Dennis said. 'But meanwhile, who knows about the arrest of Mr Mischkov, Arthur? Has an announcement been made?'

'Not yet, Dennis,' Arthur said. 'Quite a scoop, eh? Like the old days. Usual terms?'

'Usual terms,' Dennis said. 'Just give me the details.'

'Just like that?' Becky said. 'No wonder no one's got faith in the police or the press!'

'Come on, Mum!' Jonathan said. 'It's Christmas! Can Jazz come to this New Year's Eve party?'

'What, and be bored by a load of drunken old farts ruining the lawn with their dog-ends? Surely the two of you will have something better to do? If not, of course she's welcome. Everyone is, even you and Susan, Dennis.

And Harold, naturally. Though it might not be as exciting as this one.'

'Just give me the address, ma'am,' Arthur said, 'and I'll see if I can arrange a police raid. Would that help?'

Becky gave him a look that would normally turn her actors' knees to water. Then she burst out laughing. 'Why not?' she said. 'We all like surprises, don't we?' And she took a truffle and popped it into her mouth.

DEAD *Sharp.*

DEAD *Funny.*

DEAD *Good.*

The Pumpernickel Mysteries

Crime with heart, humour . . . *and a poodle.*

The Pumpernickel Mysteries Series

Leo Wengrowski runs a one-man-and-a-dog legal practice in London's Soho.

Pumpernickel, a standard black poodle, is the dog. They are both in their seventies; the dog has more hair. Leo's partner is Dr Marion Fitzwalter, a psychotherapist with an international reputation who is a couple of years older, and a couple of inches taller, than Leo, though as he says it makes no difference when they're lying down.

Leo's oldest friend is Dennis Arbuthnot, 'the world's most fearless crime reporter', who has extensive contacts among both the police and the criminal world.

Leo provides legal advice to victims and those suspected of violent crimes, Marion helps people with messed-up minds, Dennis rubbishes Leo's attempts to act like a detective but occasionally provides inside information. Pumpernickel acts as a sounding-board for Leo's ideas, offers reassurance to his nervous clients, and can sniff out drugs, disease, and dishonesty.

Four veterans who are still working, still learning, still arguing, still loving life and each other, and still able to surprise the younger generations who come to them with their problems. Problems that are often in today's headlines, including the oldest headline of all: murder.